Analysis of a Natural Terraform (A.N.T.)

**Book One
of the
Terraform Trilogy**

Tereska Karran

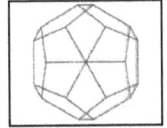

STREET PUBLISHING

Published by STREET PUBLISHING 2018

Disclaimer

This is a work of fiction. The characters and events portrayed here, other than those clearly in the public domain, are fictitious and any resemblance to real persons, living or dead, is purely coincidental.

STREET PUBLISHING

Streetpublishing.co.uk

Dedication

I would like to thank Laura and Jack for their encouragement during the writing of this book. Without them it may never have seen the light of the internet.

Contents

Introduction

The Terraform Chronicles consists of four books describing the discovery and activation of a puzzling artefact.

The first book describes its initialization. Everything we know about this is based around independent research on this curiosity undertaken by a group of university academics. The narrative includes excerpts and results from their work where relevant.

The researchers, denoted by first names, have chosen to remain anonymous although they have edited the material to ensure accuracy.

The present whereabouts of the artefact described in their work are unknown.

Prelude

The ancient car slowed before a cavernous Victorian mansion facing Clapham Common with a loud click from the handbrake. The old lady was already at the door. Her bony hands, outstretched to hug her granddaughter, were almost transparent, revealing blue corded veins.

A tiny child pressed her wrists against the glass of the car window and waved to the old lady. A network of blue veins showed through her skin. Grandmama's was blue, and that was bad.

"Hurry up," said her mother irritably.

Mama had red communist blood, which hadn't stopped her from being shipped to the Siberian gulags. She and grandmama Renia had escaped the gulags together. They disagreed on everything, though they had forged a fragile alliance so that Lucia had somewhere to go during school holidays.

"Hello, darling granddaughter."

The two women kissed each other on the cheeks.

Grandmama's long hair was wound around her head in two plaits, like a crown. She was wearing the same outfit as ever – worn tweed riding skirt, a knit waistcoat and brogues. She stood by the door and nodded as they entered, closing the massive stained-glass door behind her disdainfully. Mama wore flannel trousers and a pink shirt, her hair was bobbed short and she wore a gold brooch, a fox head on a riding crop.

"I can't stay long, I'm afraid," said her daughter, "I have to catch up on housework and prepare for work tomorrow."

Renia bowed her head slightly, as befitted a princess and the rightful heir to vast estates in what was now the Ukraine.

The old lady's Russian family had been pushed to the Ukraine after the revolution and then exiled by Stalin's expansion. She clung onto as many of the old ways as possible. She and other refugees formed their own threadbare version of society. Her house was full of threadbare antiques - outlandish items with claw feet and mother of pearl inlay, jewel coloured Persian Rugs, and wonderful, transparent porcelain from the local junk shops. She had found an elderly Polish cleaning lady who worked for almost nothing. She never cooked unless Lucia was staying and usually lived on packaged food, hard boiled eggs (and caviar when she could afford it).

Lucia gave the old lady a brief hug and ran into the cavernous house. It smelled of wax polish and stewed tea. She headed for the garden while the two women held a guarded conversation over an ancient black samovar. There was a walled kitchen garden, at the end of end of the once kempt formal parterre. Lucia headed for it, checking if anything had changed since her last visit.

Nothing had. As usual, it was full of straggly overgrown exotic vegetables: asparagus, courgettes, and peculiar squashes as well as traditional vegetables. She pulled up some radishes and beets to see if they had grown, hastily replanting them when mama called her back to say goodbye.

The two women were exchanging farewells in their usual frigid fashion.

"Do not forget the past," said grandmama perfunctorily kissing her daughter, "it informs our future."

"Bah," replied mama, looking sharply at her daughter warningly (to ensure she wasn't imbibing counter revolutionary ways). "Obliterate the past ... Build a new world."

She turned to her daughter. "I'll come by next weekend," she gave her a brief hug, "phone in the evenings when I'm back from work." She held her daughter closer. "And don't listen to the old lady," she whispered. "She doesn't mean any harm, she's just retrograde."

"I'll be back soon," she said loudly. "Keep in touch. You have my number ... blah ..."

Lucia hugged her mother tight. "I love you mummy," she said.

Mama did not reply. The front door closed on her school and her daily term time regimen. The holidays had begun.

§

Lucia settled into her holiday way of life. Grandmama had looked after her since she was a baby, filling in for her mother when her work schedules made it impossible to deal with her daughter.

"What shall we do today granny? Can we go for a walk? Can we go to the shops?" She bounced around, already bored with the old house. "Can I draw?"

Grandmama sighed and sat down by her bubbling samovar and lit a cigarette. "Run to the garden just for a moment. Run and play dear. Say hello to the chickens."

Lucia ran back to the garden, carefully avoiding the terrifying beasts for now. She grabbed a towel and returned to a place she had located earlier. It was the perfect spot to dig a small trench. After fifteen minutes of scrabbling in the soil she judged the diggings ready for the next stage - water.

There was a soft rustling from the bottom of the garden. The chickens knew she was there, just locked up.

She sang to herself as she filled it with water from an ancient brass tap and started on the next stage of her new project, a giant mud pie island. She intended to decorate it with a few overgrown vegetables in the wilderness grandmama called a vegetable garden.

Grandmama sat by the French windows. It was June, but the place was already a bit of a jungle, and she couldn't see Lucia though the dense foliage.

Grandmama had a good idea of *what* to grow, *when* it was in season, and *where* it should be planted, yet hadn't a clue *how* to grow it. Servants had done everything, while skilfully maintaining the illusion that she was in charge. Lucia often watched her cry tears of bitter, frustrated rage when something failed to grow from seed. She cried silently and privately; never in front of grownups.

The cooing from the bottom of the garden grew louder. The beasts had recognised her, and she could avoid them no longer.

She approached the fenced-off run, where chickens and geese scrabbled aimlessly at the bare earth. She checked the gate … locked. She stared at the birds warily. They stared back; first with one eye, then the other. She held a wilted beetroot plant in her hand ready for planting on her mud island.

The geese eyed it greedily.

After a brief battle of wills, both opposing forces walked away, ignoring each other.

§

Life in Clapham had its own routine. Time passed quickly. The days were relaxed and mostly uneventful. Each morning they fed the monstrous chickens, a frenzied, cooing affair. The remainder of the day was generally devoted to what grandmama deemed a "proper" country house education.

She learnt how to manage an estate. She visited other old ladies and had bitter, stewed tea. They held their own tea parties. Lucia bowed and spoke to them in French, "the language of the salon", claimed her grandmama.

They grew plants. They plucked leaves out of herbaceous borders. They visited the common and collected herbs which were used to prepare herbal remedies to dose the poor (the cleaning lady took the infusions home to her family).

"You never know when you'll need to rely on medicine like this," warned grandmama. "It saved my life and that of others countless times in Siberia."

Lucia acquired the impression that Siberia was full of sick people - and zombies - since everyone there had died.

Every few days they visited local shops to buy the tiny portions of food that the old lady lived on. This was a ritual in itself.

First, they entered the shop and said, "Good day."

Lucia curtsied. Grandmama bowed her head regally and returned the greeting in a thick accent. She spoke several languages: Russian, Polish, Russki, French (a bastard drawing-room version which would make a French person cough in polite embarrassment) and German; (Lucia suspected that she also knew chicken and bird-talk.) She never bothered to learn a word of English, which she regarded as an inferior language. She never got the hang of its rule-less order and intonation.

Then, grandmama addressed mystified shopkeepers in every tongue she knew in turn (except bird-speak, naturally), before turning to the child and ranting how stupid and uncultured they were.

Finally, with dignity and honour established, she said "Bah" and handed Lucia her pennies and instructed her to buy.

"Granny wants a packet of cigarettes, a quarter of ham and some cheddar cheese, please," said the girl while granny stood by disdainfully.

The child stood next to her relative as the transaction was completed. She found it hard not to join in the giggling of the smirking shop-keepers, who found the little charade hilarious.

And that was the pattern of the summer.

§

Except for the special days, which followed a strict pattern.

The strangeness began when grandmama Renia declared "Today is a Special Day."

Lucia shivered. How did she know?

She waited for the next words without expression, just in case grandmama changed her mind.

Grandmama put on her gardening shoes, slowly. "We-are-Feeding-the-Birds," she declared, picking up a small spade which marked out the momentous occasion. "Join us if you like."

Lucia left her toys and got up obediently. They walked through the garden in silence, grandmama stalking ahead in dignified disdain.

A rustling from the coop suggested that the huge birds knew something

10

was up. They clucked and murmured to each other at the digging tool in grandmother's hands.

The cockerel, an exotic beast, with sparkling plumage and mad eyes, established the pecking order among his harem. Fifteen or so regimented fowls nestled close; making extraordinary sounds, heads swivelling to follow the old lady's every move.

As soon as the gate was open, the war party left the coup *en masse*, scouting the garden for an ants' nest. Grandmama led the group, her eyes fixed to the ground and shifting in colour from totally green to black. She clicked and chirruped with her feathered followers.

Lucia didn't consider this odd. She ran after them, struggling to keep up, crushed among the warm plumage.

Every so often, the old lady stopped, causing a wave of chaos among the little troop. Lucia invariably fell over, and ran about panic-stricken.

"Hurry up," gloated grandmother unsympathetically, "or you'll miss the fun."

When she located an ants' nest, the old lady changed; bristling, upright, with enormous flashing eyes. She paused, poised her spade carefully, and stabbed deep into an anthill.

Mayhem! Fowls swarmed over the exposed underground hive. Ants hurled themselves at the birds' bills and eyes, stinging ferociously in defence of their young grubs. Lucia bobbed about delighted; it was like her favourite television programme, Doctor Who. The chickens stretched their necks so that their feathers stood up, making them look skinny and alien.

Grandmama, now a green-eyed warrior woman, swirled in the centre, clicking and whistling, while chickens clucked back at her and pushed each other.

The geese, which had followed at a slight distance and had so far stayed out of the proceedings, now joined in, hissing. The child bobbed about in the frenzy.

Shortly after the first cut into the soil, grandmama, who was now a regal Valkyrie-like creature, hushed the birds away.

They held back, an undulating fluffy mass, clucking and cooing.

The ants had been scurrying about frantically, trying to drag their grubs and eggs away.

Grandmama was inexorable. She stabbed the ground again, this time pulling out the queen herself. There was always a hush when this happened.

11

Even the planes and traffic around them seemed to grow silent. She stood imperious, before throwing the giant disabled insect to the ravening beasts below.

The birds now fell on the hapless ants' nest. And grandmama stood still as stone in the feathered mayhem, clicking furiously in an eerie tune. It felt epic, even though they were just feeding chickens in a Clapham garden.

Before long, it was over. The warrior woman reverted into a little, eccentrically-dressed old lady.

They walked back and had the tea and cakes grandmama had laid out earlier. She poured out tea, as if nothing had happened.

Yet it felt like a celebration.

Phase 1 - Initialisation

In which Lucia decides to visit the Ukraine, the land of her parents.

She finds her grandmother's home and locates a curious piece of rock, which she decides to bring home.

Initialisation Stage One:

First Contact

1.

The pillared campus quadrangle bathed in sunshine, its grand stepped portico littered with students and lecturers eating lunch, checking mobiles or both. It was bustling for now, but would empty as everyone headed to the exam hall for 2.00pm.

The invigilators sat slightly apart - four casually dressed and slightly scruffy men and a young, smartly dressed female. She looked out of place among the nerdy computer scientists.

Lucia was the youngest lecturer in her department, and an honorary male in the hallowed temple of science. She worked twice as hard as male colleagues for half of the recognition, though there was no overt discrimination. Staff were assessed by contributions to the RA (Research Assessment) profile).

'Properly Refereed' papers were really all that mattered in the bitter status wars of academia, although they could be about anything. (Creating a zombie epidemic was a popular topic in the biochemistry department).

§

Lucia stretched out her legs, hoping to catch a bit more daylight before she went into the darkened building while her colleagues squinted resentfully at the sun.

The rest of the group looked up at the sun resentfully.

"It's impossible to work in such heat," they complained.

Lucia was looking forward to her summer break. The last year had been particularly difficult as she managed her teaching, childcare and divorce. With two young children she'd spent the last year juggling lectures, playgroup and school all year. She took naps on the tube, between lectures, and in meetings and knew perfectly well never to mention any marriage or childcare issues.

In fact, she hadn't needed to mention the matter to her head of department until the last semester.

"Bad luck," said the professor. "I hope you're not asking for compassionate leave?"

"Of course not."

In truth, she was exhausted. The decree absolute had arrived yesterday, and she'd been out celebrating. She didn't feel like being indoors on such a lovely day. The weather was gorgeous.

The subject of research papers and conferences had been thoroughly discussed and the group turned to another subject for debate.

"What are you doing this summer?" asked Barry, her colleague. She opened her mouth to respond, but he didn't wait to hear the answer and launched on a detailed description of his projected motorcycling holiday across France. From what she could tell, it had been planned to the last detail, to the extent of setting an alarm for precisely 6.00am every morning and stopping for a break at precisely 100.00am in a chosen and pre-planned location.

She yawned, trying to catch a bit more sunshine while the rest of the group huddled in the ever-decreasing shade.

A colleague chipped in to describe his holiday and after few minutes a third interpolated his holiday plans in the gaps. Lucia tried to tune out of the conversation. It wasn't possible, they checked in now and again to make sure she was listening.

The group shrank back from the relentless sun. It beat back the shade slowly but surely, depriving them of cover. Fortunately, at the last minute the chief invigilator arrived with the key and the papers.

He was sweating profusely.

"Look at this sunshine," he complained. "How can students concentrate in bright light?"

Barry tapping his watch behind his back "late!" he muttered, "as usual." They entered the building. The chief invigilator swished a hand towards the windows and waved at Lucia, who dutifully blocked out sunlight with giant blinds. She opened windows slightly, to cool the place down with the minimum of fresh air.

He handed her the scripts, smiling patronisingly. "One per desk," he ordered, carefully watching in case she misunderstood.
She placed scripts on the desks, answer books alongside while the rest of the group sat and chatted.

Barry settled down at the back of the lecture hall. He put a wad of marking on his knee and laid out his marking pens.

"We need someone walking along the gaps between seats," explained the chief invigilator, as if she had never done this before. "Make sure that no student has anything on their desk other than the list here." Lucia glanced at it. "Of course," she acquiesced.

The students filed into the hall, placing bags at the back. The invigilator read out the exam rubric in an officious voice and the exams began.

After five minutes the invigilators went on a tea-break leaving Barry to his marking while Lucia walked up and down the aisles checking on students. The only sound in the room was the scratch of pen to paper and the click of the blinds as they swayed in the breeze from the outside.

A student put his hand up for another answer-book. As she walked along the narrow aisles of tense students, she thought about her planned vacation in the Ukraine. Grandmama was long dead. She had left her ancient sepia photographs and title documents to a grand old castle, papers she had clung to throughout her sojourn in Siberia.

("Promise me you'll go back," she had whispered almost every time she'd seen her. "Of course, granny," child Lucia had replied.)

She smiled wryly.

The visit was an act of revisionism, a tiny act of rebellion against mama. True, the place was in political and economic turmoil, although it was safe for Western Europeans to visit. After a great deal of acrimonious argument, she'd resolved to go alone, while her ex took the children to France with his new girlfriend.

She was looking forward to it.

2.

Two weeks later, an ancient plane touched down in the Carpathian Mountains. Large posters in the airport displaying dramatic scenery could not entirely overcome the military feel of the place. At least it had opened the mountains. The tourist brochure said the area was 'remote and beautiful,' full of 'exciting off-piste slopes' - in other words, it was undeveloped and highly dangerous for moderate skiers.

Lucia collected her baggage and attempted once again to contact her children. She swept the airport seeking a signal. None.

It wasn't her phone. She had a brand new one.

Deep in the heart of the Ukraine, a strange device was hi-jacking the bandwidth as it sent excited messages to the sky.

{"Arrival immanent," it declared to no one in particular}

Lucia stepped out of the airport. Just before she left, she turned to a heavily armed airport official, asking if there was a problem with the wifi signal.

"Our mobile networks are troubled by unusual electronic activity in the mountain area," he replied in a sonorous voice. "Do not be troubled. It is temporary and will be fixed."

It figured, supposed Lucia. This was a remote area and the internet had been dodgy all summer, even in England.

§

Lucia picked up her car and drove out of the airport. She waved her phone at the sky.

There'd been something wrong with the broadband for several days. Networks everywhere in the northern hemisphere were reporting interference from unknown sources.

Her phone buzzed.

She looked at her screen, a text, no sender no message. She had been getting them all morning.

If anyone had been watching the strange rock in a cabinet high in the mountains, they'd have noticed it glowing. It was using all its carefully stored power to contact its target. It made yet another attempt to communicate. It hadn't worked out the communication protocols yet and sent another blank text, no sender.

{"This way," it ordered.}

On the car seat, the phone's screen activated. The phone remained silent, uncomprehending. Lucia tapped her phone. She wanted to call her children.

"There has to be some signal," she thought irritably, or her phone wouldn't be receiving phantom calls and empty texts, but she couldn't make a call.

§

Lucia took out an ancient paper map, trying to work out where she was.

Without the careful voice of the satnav telling her where to go she was a bit lost. It wasn't just the obscure signposts directing her to mysterious places; the whole business of driving was terrifying. It involved gesticulating arguments with cars in the middle of the road and having half-understood arguments with drivers over tiny bridges. The paper map which seemed to depict the country as entirely empty bar one or two roads.

She drove through exquisite towns and villages surrounded by dramatic countryside, marred by nodding oil wells and criss-crossed by pipe-lines.

Finally, when it was almost dark, she managed to locate the area her grandmother always talked about by asking the locals, using half-forgotten words from her childhood. Several people praised her accent, although they said she spoke a weird old-school intonation.

Never mind, this was grandmama had lived.

She'd booked a room in a pretty farmhouse on the internet. Her family dacha was nearby. There was a spectacular, pretty village alongside it. It was used for village gatherings. The villagers were charmingly friendly. They were fascinated when she said who she was.

{"Close," the rock said to the skies.}

"It's nice to belong," thought Lucia.

The next day, Lucia explored the area. She talked to the locals in her broken Russki.

People knew of her grandfather. Before the area was 'revolutionised', grandfather had prospected for oil, and found it. He had built a model village for the oil workers, who mostly resented his interference and called him a tyrant, but in a nice way.

She drove to a little gothic town not far from the village. It was appealing, with an empty plinth at one end, sporting Lenin's feet. At the other end there was a church which matched the palace in turret and ornament.

She ventured and got into a conversation with the Roman Catholic priest. She explained that her grandparents came from the area. They spoke a mixture of languages and managed to make sense to each other. It seemed that he knew a lot about the palace, having been born in the local village. He was a keen local historian and was delighted to show her round. As soon as he learnt who she was he directed her to the monuments to her family.

"Do you know that resemble your great grandmother?" he pointed to a painting of a tall lady with long blond hair in two plaits over her tomb.

Lucia was suitably flattered.

He directed her to her great grandfather Prince Augustin's last resting place. It was in a glass coffin under the Altar of the Presence. The prince had no doubt thought a lot of himself; and his body was embalmed. Lucia recalled grandmama's careful instructions on how to prepare a banquet and manage a great estate. Her stories of a grand life in the Ukraine were true after all.

She lifted the white lace tablecloth covering the glass coffin. The corpse was desiccated, with long hair and fingernails, which must have grown after he was dead. He looked like a vampire, or giant insect, with extraordinary elongated shoulder blades, like wings.

"Why does he look like that?" She asked.

"He was local-," replied the old man cryptically, "one of us."

She got no more from him.

3.

Over the next few days Lucia met the residents, who appeared to have learnt English at the same school, greeted her with the same refrain:

"How do you do? Are you well? What is weather like today?" followed by (without a pause) "It is raining, it is shining, it sunshine."

Lucia always nodded and replied "Yes, it is lovely day. I am fine, thank you".

They then shook hands and hugged, Russian style, without smiling.

She hoped to meet their teacher one day, and complain.

A few of the more ancient villagers remembered her family and cackled at her proprietarily, saying things she did not understand about faeries and little people. The rest assumed she was coming to buy things, which were all priced in dollars, overvalued, and mostly crap.

"This special 100 dollars" was the starting price for everything.

Most villagers lived in ugly, square concrete high rises close to the oil wells. Everyone had an equal amount of space in either the new model village, or the communal farm. It was allocated by the village and works commissariat and completely fair. There were excellent gyms and sports facilities. Most people seemed to live indoors all the time, or underground, away from the sun.

The flats were damp and unprepossessing. They smelt of cabbage and garlic. The inhabitants appeared fat and beefy yet pale and wan. Their children had a dull faces of children lacking stimulus. The height of local ambition was to work in heavy industry or in a technical area such as chemical research. Anyone with a supervisory job at the refinery was particularly respected.

She met the local intelligentsia and drank with local officials. They sang songs into deep baritones until early in the morning ending up crying, hugging each other and talking meaningless babble in lugubrious tones.

It was during one of these evenings that she met the local mining engineer.

Tomasz was different from the rest. For a start he was slim and not a heavy drinker. He was tall and handsome in a military, square-headed way. He earned a pittance from his profession, though he had one of the highest salaries in the area. He was unquestionably one of the elites, a ruler in that superficially equal world. He supplemented his income by opening a cafe in the centre of the village.

Tomasz's wife was fashionable and trendy, and worked industriously to make the cafe successful. Most young people came there at one time or another. There was music from an old juke box, which played ancient Beatles and Rolling Stones and modern Moscow rock bands. On Fridays and Saturdays there was live music from an accordion, guitar and violin. Locals danced energetically and twirled Lucia around even though she was twice as tall as them.

§

Lucia asked him about the old family castle and he arranged for her visit. So it was that three days after her arrival, she drove through the old gates at the wheel of a battered old hire car.

The palace was indeed rather grand. It looked rather like a place from a fairy-tale, set in a magnificent park. The gates were topped in gothic-looking arms – the escutcheon weirdly included ants and swords. Renia had left her a signet ring with the same arms; which she wore occasionally. She never wore it – so elitist.

The palace was beautiful, in a vampire movie sort of way. There were dragon-headed gutters and giant ornate brass doors, like something from a vampire movie. No deer or fancy birds roamed the grounds; the stables functioned as a pony-trekking business for locals.

She rang on the door, expecting a gloomy death knell to sound. There was a cheerful electronic 'ding dong' instead.

A couple of nurses on lunch break greeted her cheerfully. They knew who she was.

The castle had been converted to a sanatorium during the communist era, a place where Nomenklatura (high-ranking communist officials) could recuperate after their exertions. It had been slowly falling into disuse and was almost empty. It was likely to be sold off and converted into a hotel.

The interior was lavish; in the Romanov bijou style- a Party member's guilty dream. It had a stuffy and institutional ambience, but it had survived. It had been used as a rest home for fire-fighters and policemen from Chernobyl. A few remained, in a separate wing. It was almost deserted, yet still staffed.

The senior nurse handed her over to the caretaker, who was a huge fat fellow with a heavy limp. She tried hard not to think of him as Igor. He took her around the parental pile and offered her horrific and ugly institution furniture at inflated prices in a loud stage whisper. Some of the original furniture remained and he pointed it out.

"This here 100 years," he said.

They entered a great hall containing glass cases and ancient brass engineering instruments. Some rock specimens caught her eye.

She hadn't realised grandfather had been a prospector, although thinking about it, it *was* logical. The cases were full of gemstones, fossils and geological specimens. They were covered in dust and mostly standard stuff. A lot of cases were empty. The valuable material had been removed.

She was taken around musty rooms full of specimens of local rock. It was important to show little interest and despise anything she wanted in front of the caretaker. He was unquestionably going to rip her off if he could.

She'd been trying to think what to bring for her children, and suddenly had a bright idea. She decided to take a few rock specimens home. After all, they liked the rocks in the Geological Museum in London.

There was a brief flash of light, as a one exhibit gleamed in the sun. It held her gaze.

Myriad thoughts flashed through her brain, somehow involving chickens and grandmother's weird eyes.

The rock sent a pulse of excitement through the bandwidth, knocking out the local base station and almost downing an airliner flying overhead.

{"Contact."}

4.

The rock was angular, perfectly symmetrical, and about 25 centimetres in diameter. The shape was neither carved nr finished. It had an unusual surface: matt, yet iridescent, as if it were alive. She knew instantly that she wanted it, particularly when told that it was a common local stone.

She felt in some strange way that she was meant to have it. She remembered how people talked about connection to certain crystals. Somehow this particular rock was calling to her.

The rock buzzed expectantly. It had been waiting for eons.

Lucia stared at the stone. She heard a buzzing noise. Her vision flashed in a migraine-like way.

The rock rebooted an ancient protocol. Its surface shimmered and moved around hypnotically.

{"Greetings. The perfect subject."}

She stood still, fascinated, until the caretaker took her by the arm and walked her away.

She couldn't stop talking about the weird rock.

"Where did it come from?"

The caretaker was shifty and evasive. He didn't seem sure of its provenance.

"Are there any more like it?"

"Yes, there are more."

No, he wasn't prepared to explain where. He did not know.

"Please do not ask. I cannot tell you. I do not know."

He left her at the door of the palace and almost ran off.

§

Lucia meandered back to her lodgings, mesmerised by the stone. She considered taking it home, but suspected it might be radioactive or poisonous. She resolved to ask Tomasz for more details before starting negotiations. She trusted him. His educated Russian was easy to understand, and he accepted her as equal, despite being more important than she could ever hope to be.

5.

Lucia met Tomas at the café the following morning. She mentioned the rock, which he immediately recognised from her description.

"Oh yes, most interesting," he acknowledged, "Your grandfather took a terrific risk moving it."

Lucia took a step back.

("Radioactive," she thought, "I hope I haven't spent too long in its presence.")

"The locals are credulous and regard those particular rocks as magic. There's a cave full of them nearby. The local coven meets there. It's regarded as the home of the "krasnoludy" (little people). They believe all sorts of superstitious nonsense."

They exchanged a scientific grin at superstition of all kinds.

"I've been there. It's a wonderful place," he continued, "definitely not natural, possibly Neolithic or something. The rocks *are* beautiful. I tried to bring one back to the lab. Unhappily, I nearly had a revolt on my hands and I gave up. It's of no geological interest. It's meant to be unlucky to touch or move them. I believe they were processed in Neolithic times or thereabouts. I tried to examine them, but folk traditions are strong. I'm not *that* interested."

("That's it," she decided, "I'm bringing it home.")

{"Correct," communicated the rock, creating an unpleasant reverberation in Lucia's brain.}

"Augustin saw himself as an innovator, bringing the 20th century to ignorant peasants. He cleared the entrance to the cave. Locals had known about it for generations and reached it by another route. It's part of a larger complex with interconnecting tunnels. We can explore them if you like..."

Her smile froze; she hated caving.

{"Go there. Yes!!" screeched the rock.}

Something tugged at Lucia, urging her to visit...
Her phone buzzed - another random empty text.
"Maybe I should go there?" she thought.
"Anyway," rambled Tomasz obliviously, "old Augustin took the rock out

of the cave and brought it home for his exhibition. The locals were sure he would drop dead - he just laughed."

Lucia nodded; she remembered tough old grandmama Renia, who was afraid of nothing except losing face.

"He opened the caves, which caused colossal fuss."

He blinked as if recollecting something extraordinary.

"That was the first recorded outbreak of the unique deformities common around here."

{"Go!!"}

"We represent the people here" he persevered in a smug, flat voice, "and *respect* local customs and culture."

He blinked again (a sure sign he was hiding something).

"The prince's youngest boy fell in love with a local girl and killed himself. Locals insisted it was bad luck for moving the boulder. When communists liberated the area, the old man was shot, and his family shipped to Siberia - that was the rock too."

{"Go!!"}

She was excited.

"Can you take me to the cave?" she begged.

There was a pause.

"The matter is delicate. We need to tread carefully. I'm not sure where it is. The little people are taken seriously, and we need to find someone pretty foolhardy to guide us."

{"Find them. It will change everything."}

Tomasz had been speaking in a droning voice, almost as if he had thought through the story of the rocks and the cave before and come to a decision not to interfere with local superstition. Lucia's keenness to visit the site made him rethink the matter. There was a long silence as he came to a decision.

"Of course," he said in an urbane voice. "The area is not off limits."

Lucia looked at him suspiciously.

His face was bland, open.

"All the same, I will come with you. You've revived my interest in the place. I'll ask around. What about Monday afternoon?"

"Of course," she accepted, imagining herself on the brink of archaeological discovery, fame and fortune. Then she remembered the garden in Clapham and the chickens, her grandmama's weird eyes and chirruping voice. She recalled reading about peasant beliefs in witchcraft, divination, hallucinogenic mushrooms and little people. She gave into a little trill of fear.

"What about these little people? Everyone seems to talk about them. Maybe there is something bad about the place. What exactly are little people anyway?" She spoke with disdain mixed with a tiny trace of fear.

The engineer observed her carefully. He didn't want to imply that he was ignorant and superstitious.

"Just little people." he muttered.

"In Britain," she encouraged him, "they're believed to have power for good or evil. They cause bad luck, curdle milk and so on."

"The same thing exactly," he agreed, brightening. "They also cause miscarriages and abnormalities. They're feared and only *baba yaga*[1] go near them. They aren't scared, "cos they're deformed anyway."

"You make them sound like genetic engineers," she laughed.

{"Genetic Engineers. Correct."}

Tomasz laughed rather hollowly and blinked.

"When Augustin moved the rock, there was a spate of miscarriages and birth defects."

He was quiet for a moment.

"It hasn't abated. They've gone for further study ..." he stopped and cleared his throat, "for study in Moscow."

He chose his words carefully.

"The old prince was hated for opening that cave. There is some mysterious deformity causing mineral here. It's probably pollution in the water uncovered by mining operations - villagers just don't see it that way."

----

[1] A woman with supernatural powers in Slavic myth, deemed to have magic skills.

Lucia smiled. Tomasz represented the new order, while actually sympathising with the old.

"The villagers didn't support the prince when he prospected for oil," explained Tomasz. "He had to hire outsiders. He got cheated and progress was slow." A look of commiseration came over his face. "It delayed everything. *We* don't mess with local customs."

"Is there any danger?"

"None from the caves, although there *are* malformations in the village." He hesitated before he spoke, "some of them are most peculiar."

(Lucia changed her mind. "No way am I taking it home," she thought, "it's some unknown chemical, and dangerous. Don't mess with it.")

"What's this stone got to do with birth defects?"

"Ho, ho," he jeered, "cursed stones, my foot. Call yourself civilised Westerner? You're as superstitious as any villager."

"So it's nothing to do with the rocks?"

"Nothing at all. They're local sedimentary rock with an oily finish, probably Neolithic, and not at all interesting. I checked it for radiation and poisons when I first saw it. The little people are a mask for local covens - very vicious they are too. They mix potions which contain poisons, no doubt the root of these birth defects." He looked down at his hands. "Local babas take drugs which make them ugly as sin," he mentioned, "long noses, wild, dry brittle hair."

Lucia smoothed her hair down, hoping it was behaving.

"It's not just magic mushrooms. There's a lot to the old herbs that scientists are just beginning to uncover. For instance, plants and herbs are influenced by the phases of the moon..."

"The birth defects," she interrupted. She knew how the Eastern European psyche combined folk myths with science. "They can't be caused by witches surely, or they'd be burnt at the stake."

"That's why they blame little people of course," he replied.

"Still," he continued, "I'd love to know which drug, or combination of herbs, causes some of the more inexplicable defects. Claws and carapaces, exo-skeletons, mandibles, we can't guess what causes them. What causes a baby to look like an insect, another species altogether?"

"Horrible," she mumbled to herself. "Sounds like the Fly."

6.

Nothing occurred to delay the expedition.

The next Monday at 7.00 am Tomasz and a young female guide arrived, ready to hike to the caves.

Lucia shook hands with the unsmiling girl, who was a little cross-eyed, signifying second 'sight' and one of the local signs of a baba...

They set off uphill at a sharp pace, trekking through unspoilt countryside, untouched by farming or industrialisation. About halfway up a low mountain, there was a group of caves, set in a cliff where mountains had split away, with a footpath cut into the steep rock face.

The path was steep, unrailed and headily dangerous. Lucia had to sit down several times, groggy in the thin air and determined not to look down at the steep fall.

"There's a system of interconnecting tunnels throughout the mountainside," Tomasz explained, "as yet unexplored."

He glanced significantly at the guide.

As they got closer it was clear that Tomasz was right; the caves couldn't be natural. The main cavern was perfectly round in an area where rocks were sharp and craggy. Yet it appeared to be bored through solid rock with smooth, even polished, sides. It was perfectly round.

When the party reached it at last, almost dragging Lucia with them, the preternatural smoothness of the cave walls was even more obvious.

It looked polished, and the walls shone with speckles like a fake granite kitchen countertop.

They stopped at the mouth of the largest cave, which was dry and airy. The floor was smooth and looked paved. There was no debris, no sand, no signs of animal or plant life. It contained ten geometrically shaped rocks laid out in a circle - nothing else.

The countryside fell silent around them. It seemed as if an observant darkness surrounded them. The stones in the cave were awake, watchful...

Maugosia whistled a specific tuneless phrase.

{"Friend or foe?" whispered the stones.}

Maugosia whistled again - 'Friend.'

{"Friend or foe?" they screeched into the skies.}

Their sentinels had gone. The skies were empty, and they were alone.
Maugosia whistled once more, reassuringly.
The stones settled down to wait.

§

"Well, here we are," said Tomasz nonchalantly.
His voice echoed through the caves unpleasantly.
"As you see there's nothing here."
The area was dry and swept clean. The walls were glassy and black, like mirrored obsidian.
Lucia touched a Rock. It felt light. The sound of her hand across its surface echoed in her mind like an itch.
"These are interesting," she offered, "perhaps I'll take one home."
She kicked one lightly with her foot.
"They seem very light, possibly pumice stone ..."
She took off her rucksack and attempted to lift the one nearest to the entrance.
An electric shock stung through her arm.
She jumped back, almost hitting the dark walls of the cavern.
"Static?" She said.
Her head felt light and dizzy. She felt rather than saw movement and there was a strange noise in her ears. There *was* something there, almost a presence.
And Maugosia, a baba yaga after all, went mad. Spitting curses, she revealed herself as protector of the cave.
"Do not touch the stones, they are sacred, and can kill. I am called to defend them from ignorance."
Lucia felt confused, floating, as if she was underwater. She could see rather than feel the girl dragging at her arm frantically.
"Why are you shouting?" she wondered, "What's going on? Is something wrong?"
Tomasz was trying to calm Maugosia.
He too, was shouting. Lucia could feel the vibrations of his words without really hearing them.
"You can never tell with backward-looking peasants," he apologised to Lucia.

His voice echoed her brain, reverberating, as if from a distance. He was trying to reassure Maugosia, telling her that the rock would be properly studied in Britain, by respected lecturers. There was money at her university for the study of such scientific phenomena. It might be an important artefact.

No use. Maugosia insisted that the rocks could not be moved or even touched.

Tomasz dragged at her sleeve. The girl wouldn't budge; she seemed ready to die for the place.

The stones were idle, boding gently at the skies. Lucia sensed that they were communicating something.

{"There are limited supplies of venom," said one.}

{"True, and the female provides a sufficient defence," responded another, in an almost audible whirr.}

Lucia could just about hear Tomasz and the girl arguing over the buzzing in her head, but she did not did not take part.

The world had slowed down. She felt as if she was falling slowly into another universe where verticality meant nothing. She was floating in space.

Gradually, things sped up. She could understand the argument going on around her.

It seemed that Tomasz was an important figure in the town and village.

"We can arrest you and your family, disappear you and obliterate your memory," he insisted, his voice ringing unpleasantly through the empty space.

Maugosia nodded, admitting his power. She was obviously scared, yet still defended the cave and its contents.

"The stones are in *my* sacred care," she said in a wavering voice. "The elders will kill me anyway. I have no choice."

Lucia listened to the discussion wearily.

Tomasz claimed a connection with the secret police. It was possible, Lucia decided. Some of his threats sounded old school, although he *might* have been playing on the girl's fears.

"We'll certify you as a mental case," he shouted. "You cannot prevent scientific progress."

The girl refused to back down.

"The cave will be investigated whether you like it or not. I only need to report back on this and the cave will be filled with concrete."

It was only then that the girl released the one from the palace. She stood up straight from her bowed and servile position. She glanced at the stones around her and spoke with a seer's voice, looking like a heroine in an old black and white movie. She chanted and whistled at the rocks, which glimmered strangely in the light from outside.

Finally, she turned to the scientists.

"The one in the palace will travel abroad," she said.

She turned away from them and seemed to be addressing something living in the cave. She nodded at something or someone.

"Yes, I'll see to it myself."

Tomasz was unimpressed. He grabbed her.

"What's going on?"

Maugosia pulled away, gabbling nonsense about magic interspersed with clicks and insect-like screeches and sing-song dirges.

Tomasz shook her.

She shook him off.

"I am keeping you safe. These are protective songs from long ago," she alleged.

Lucia watched the scene disinterestedly, feeling as if she was high above, looking down on the arguing pair. She sensed that deep inside the cave, something was watching them.

She couldn't believe it. Instead, she felt sure it was just some kind of hallucinatory experience and suspected Maugosia of drugging them.

{"We are safe," said one of the Guardians.}

{"For now," agreed the others.}

Tomasz was furiously berating the girl, he refused to be intimidated by the mystic nonsense and moved to strike her down.

Lucia intervened weakly.

"Just let her do her thing."

She felt sick and dizzy.

After a while, Maugosia stopped chanting.

Tomasz marched the girl to a ledge close to the mouth of the cave, keeping an authoritative hand on her shoulder. He sat her down, looming over her threateningly.

"These stones have power," said Maugosia, turning to Lucia with composure. "Take the rock from the house."

Tomasz growled at her, "We'll take anything we want."

Maugosia ignored him.

"The rock you are taking is weak. It is better for you. Take good care of it."

Lucia stared at her, confused. Was she receiving instructions on the care of a rock?

She felt faint. ('It has to be the altitude,' she decided.)

Maugosia looked at her sympathetically,

"Look after it well." She grabbed Lucia's hand and hugged her dramatically, and whispered a message. "Take care, if stones are provoked, disaster will result."

Lucia wasn't sure if she understood.

"Rock care?" she repeated, befuddled. ('I must be hallucinating. They've given me something … fly agaric or something.')

"Take care of it." The girl repeated, squeezing her hand. "The rocks give off emanations."

"Emanations?" said Lucia. ('I don't understand. Maybe the word means something else? I don't really speak this language.')

She sat herself down at a small distance from the girl feeling disoriented.

Tomasz paced about furiously while Lucia held her head in her hands, trying to focus.

"The girl is mad," he muttered. "This is primitivism. It must be eradicated for the country to make progress."

Further within the cave the Stones buzzed, almost within the range of hearing, enough to make both Lucia and Tomasz extremely uneasy.

Maugosia was unfazed.

"Renia was one of us," she berated Lucia, "she *knew*. She protected the cave. She *listened*."

After about five minutes, Lucia's head cleared.

She stood up.

"I feel fine. It's just the altitude."

She gathered her wits and stepped towards the cave. She stopped almost immediately. Her head was spinning, and she felt odd again. 'This is a nightmare.'

For some reason. she was once again reminded of grandmama, and the garden at Clapham during her childhood. She had a heart-sinking recollection of her grandmother talking to birds, and even ants.

She turned to her companions.

"Maybe we should return. It'll get dark. I'm not sure I can handle the altitude."

Irritatingly, Maugosia was still giving advice on rock care.

"If they're wrongly disturbed," the girl advised, "children and animals will be born dead, or early, or much worse." she gabbled instructions in Russki, insisting that Tomasz explain.

Tomasz shouted her down.

"Shut up! This is ignorance."

Lucia looked at the girl closely. Maybe her eyes would go green? She almost asked Maugosia if she spoke to ants too.

Tomasz was bearing up really well, still logical, still trying to get the situation under control. Whatever this was, it wasn't affecting him.

"We can take the stones out of the cave if we want to," he insisted, stamping his foot. "We can do anything in the interests of Science."

He gave Maugosia a threatening look and marched deeper into the cave.

At once the noise returned, reverberating through the cave. The buzzing grew increasingly audible. The silence in the cave was only a prayer, drowning out the distant sound of birdsong.

Lucia's head felt like it was going to explode.

Maugosia shouted a warning.

Tomasz paused.

Abruptly, the hum from the mouth of the cave subsided.

Tomasz slowed, relented, took a step back and retreated with dignity.

"Don't worry," he said in a smug voice, "we won't touch your precious rocks. Lucia can take the one at the palace."

Tension left the air. All was rural bliss. They could hear the birds and the rustling leaves. It was peaceful again, as if something had departed.

Maugosia stomped around, whistling and clicking her tongue. Lucia and Tomasz exchanged glances and he shrugged his shoulders. It was a local madness, albeit, the scary and frightening kind that you didn't laugh off.

{"They will be left alone" agreed the stones.}

The girl looked a little dejected and very tired.

"You can go in now. Only don't touch anything," she said. "Just take a look around."

They stepped back into the cave.

All was quiet.

The rocks surrounded them, boding gently, somehow appearing alive, and even - malevolent.

Lucia took photographs, standing well away from the uniquely shaped rocks, and taking care not to brush against them. Tomasz accompanied her. He too kept well away from the rocks.

Miraculously, for the type of scientists who blundered into million-year-old curses and fell into potholes, their innate survival instincts had kicked in. They avoided million-year old traps and vials of poison which littered the place.

§

After about an hour, they had completed their brief survey of the cave and trekked downhill in silence.

Lucia returned to her lodgings.

She saw Tomasz in a new light and was not sure she liked him. She was homesick for boring England and sorry she'd committed to moving the rock.

7.

The incident in the caves had cost Lucia her popularity in the village. Over the next week she tried to back down from removing the Rock to the UK (in a dignified and educated sort of way).

Tomasz wasn't having it. He needed to exert his authority. He took Lucia to the old palace where the Rock was officially handed over.

The caretaker led them forward into the dank chamber.

He slowly opened the glass cabinet, looking as if he was holding his breath. The old man was wearing heavy duty gloves and a leather apron. He carefully slid the object into a cardboard box, under Tomasz's watchful eye. He wrapped it in brown paper and tied it carefully with string. Tomasz observed with folded arms and a grim smile on his face.

Lucia took the package gingerly. She didn't *want* to take it, but her scientific-self yelled at her to stop being so superstitious.

It was surprising light. It might be hollow...

She had gone over the cave incident in her mind the night before handover. It had to be altitude sickness. After all, it was 2,500 metres and she lived in London, almost at sea level. She berated herself for being a weakling and resolved to join a gym at home.

§

The incident seemed like such a small thing, yet it rendered the remainder of her stay uneasy. The longer she stayed in the village the more she was aware of whispers and gossip around the rock and her visit to the caves. There were creepy undercurrents which she didn't understand.

The expedition had revealed that the village was split between traditionalists and modernists. And both factions treated her differently. Traditionalists pattered prayers and crossed themselves as she walked past while modernists kissed her on both cheeks as a comrade and equal.

And Tomasz, he was not what he seemed. He was some kind of secret police officer or something. He had changed completely. After the visit he had spent time and energy expediting the removal in order to show he was boss. Lucia suspected it was mostly because Maugosia had shown him up.

§

After further adventures, mostly consisting of bribing people she never saw and probably didn't exist, the sample from the great house was loaded into the back of her hired car together with heaps of valueless kitsch peasant woodwork.

Lucia started the car, waving to a few friends who had come to see her off, Tomasz and his wife among them. As she drove off, waving to her friends and promising to keep in touch, a curtain twitched in the window of a house nearby. She was sure it was Maugosia.

As she drove down the road she reflected on her visit. She was glad she hadn't brought the children.

Deep within the boot of her car, the Rock activated its operating systems, dormant for the last thirty years.

{"On the way," twittered the rock to the sky.}

No one heard, although satellites above reported interference and televisions in Europe were useless for a while.

The remaining stones waited quietly in their cave.

{"Reinitialising," they declared.}

§

The rest of the holiday went by in a whirl. Lucia toured a few more places, visited the historic sites, and stayed in several villages.

Nothing matched the experience of the rock.

She felt its presence as it sat in her boot through the rest of the vacation ominous and somehow, brooding.

§

Finally, it was over. Lucia drove to the airport through beautiful countryside punctuated by unsightly heavy industry and hideous communist buildings. For no obvious reason, she felt a sense of achievement.

As she left her car and went to board the plane she felt overwhelmed by the immense, remote mountains, still visible in the wide glass windows.

"I'm glad to be leaving. It's a bit like living in a remote Scottish village where werewolves hunt on full moon," she thought, "and on a full moon."

She'd made good friends in the first week at her grandmother's place. It was welcoming and friendly, but by the second week the locals had revealed a new side. And it was all due to the infernal visit to the caves.

Something had happened there, she was sure of it. Was it a Second World War experiment? It was something strange she was sure of that.

Her head still ached after the experience and she heard clicks and strange noises, which she decided was tinnitus.

Lurking in her suitcase, the rock probed her memories and laid plans.

Initialisation Stage Two:

Infiltration

1.

Lucia was delighted to return to London, although she didn't feel well. She had a headache and some kind of tinnitus. There was an intermittent buzzing in her ears which caused her to shake her head. It was like an itch in the brain.

She picked up her suitcase, ready to catch a cab home.

Something held her back.

Her hand luggage contained her passport, her makeup bag, toothbrush, and the rock.

She wavered.

"Maybe the rock really is dangerous?" she mused.

Things had certainly become weird after the visit to the caves. Her mind teetered on the edge of abandoning it, somewhere like a wheelie bin. After all that trouble getting it home, it seemed like a bit of a waste.

It was probably best to leave the thing at work. No one would be in except for a few diehard researchers. Maybe one of them would do the investigations. It looked like a geological anomaly, so she hoped that a geology researcher working for her friend Terry might take it.

She'd emailed her colleague Terry in the geology department while still on holiday.

He had already agreed to take the rock off her hands.

She'd informed Tomasz of her decision, in the best traditions of scientific enquiry.

She phoned the department line from the airport.

Terry was in!

"I've brought the geological specimen I'd like you to look at."

"The one you emailed me about? It looked marginally interesting. Bring it over and I'll take a look when I have a moment."

"Can I bring it over now?"

"Okay, then, bring it along. I've just set up a new project and need some test materials."

"A new testing rig? Sounds interesting ... I've got that strange rock I told you about. I ought to mention that it has a reputation in the Ukraine, for being haunted or something. I'd love you to investigate ..."

"Ha ha, Lucia, it had better not turn out to be white quartz crystals or something."

"No, definitely not," said Lucia fingers crossed.

"Well, as long as it's something a bit interesting … this is the latest lab equipment. We've been working on it for 5 years and the latest version has just come in, part of my EU project. I don't want to waste my time on magic crystals."

"Promise it's not white quartz …can I bring it over and you just take a look?" she paused.

"When?"

"Now?"

There was a pause.

"Okay."

Lucia heaved a sigh of relief as she wheeled her baggage to the left luggage lockers. She grabbed the carefully wrapped parcel containing the Rock and transferred it to a large tote. She could feel the parcel humming, which was vaguely unsettling.

The airport lights flickered behind her as she left the airport and hailed a cab straight to the university.

She stalwartly refused to admit fear as she watched the familiar landscape whizz by.

"Haunted indeed! White quartz! Fairy Stones!" she muttered to herself. "What nonsense! I'm doing this in the interests of proper research! I am a Scientist after all".

§

She unloaded the bag from the cab at the stairs of the brutalist concrete and glass building which housed the university technical departments. The place was reassuringly solid, dull, boring.

There were a new set of porters at the desk and she had to sign in. The atmosphere was musty and reassuringly real. She headed straight for the Geology labs and knocked on the doors.

"Hi, Lucia," Terry said as she walked in bearing the rock, "had a good summer?

"Hi," she almost hugged him. "It's great to be back."

She felt as if she had been away for aeons, but Terry hadn't changed a bit, still refreshingly Hibernian, with a round, red face topped by an orange mop of hair.

"So," he hugged her, "you went prospecting?"

He was reassuringly dressed in his usual dirty faded jeans with a faded grey tee shirt and Doc Marten boots - the same outfit he wore every day of the year despite the fact it was summer.

He watched her sharply as she unwrapped the rock, which had thankfully stopped humming. He observed the parcel owlishly and Lucia knew that she would be in serious trouble if it was some common rock.

Terry was immensely clever and sharp-witted, and she hoped she hadn't made a fool of herself. His round spectacles did little to mitigate the working-man look, but she knew he would be scathing if the rock turned out to be something common.

Lucia mutely handed him the rock.

"It's so nice of you to agree to do it," she said diffidently.

He picked it up and tossed it from hand to hand.

"It's very light for its size," he commented. He gave it a gentle tap. It seemed to reverberate oddly. He dropped it sharply, feeling it move in his hands. "And quite unlike anything I've seen before."

"Thank goodness it's not a piece of stray uranium," she laughed looking around.

Everything in the dusty lab looked almost the same, substantial rock specimens and highly concentrated acids in jars... except for... a brand-new piece of equipment shining in the corner.

Terry didn't bat an eyelid.

"Doesn't look it."

He took the rock and threw it to one side nonchalantly.

"I haven't got a lot of time now. I'll investigate it when I can. I don't normally take in rock samples but this one sounded interesting.

"I can analyse and date it too, if you like." He pointed at the shiny new machine. "It costs several thousands to test any sample," he grinned and shrugged his shoulders, "research money. I'll do it... as you're a friend."

He fiddled with innumerable dials and tapped the touch screen on the computer.

"Look at this baby," he said proudly, "it can date any rock and is the result of years of research. It will revolutionise geology."

'Revolution is a bit of a strong word.' thought Lucia.

Nevertheless, she smiled excitedly, and showed an interest in the dusty machine, thinking ruefully how she thought of her contribution to research equally life changing.

"I ought to mention that it might be poisonous," she added. She felt obligated to mention that there was talk of emanations from the caves. "They might have infected the rock."

Terry had already forgotten the thing as he polished the lenses and switches on his creation.

"Oh, that thing. What makes you think that?"

Lucia shifted uncomfortably. Such opinions seemed out of place in a university.

"It's more what the locals think than anything provable," she said.

Terry picked up a piece of uranium from a shelf above him and handed it to her.

"No worries," he said, "this is uranium 238, probably mostly safe. We keep a lot of supposedly toxic materials here. Emanations don't kill anyone."

Lucia smiled, thoroughly reassured. If Terry said Uranium 238 was safe, it was obviously all right. She felt secure. She had returned to the invulnerable temple of science.

Terry was nice about her fears. They chatted about the vacation. They agreed that although visiting remote locations was fun, it was not a patch on the excitement of research. University life was all-encompassing and irreplaceable.

"A few of us are going for drinks this evening," said Terry. "Wanna come along?"

Lucia really wanted to go. It would be nice to get back into college life. However, she hadn't even seen her children yet. Somehow, dropping the rock off had seemed the most important thing to do.

"I can't," she replied, "I haven't even been home yet. I got back from the Ukraine this morning. My case is still in the car. I've got to get home and unpack."

"Whew, dedication."

She couldn't tell him that she had to pick up her children. No one knew she had any. Not even him. She glanced at the Rock. For some reason she felt guilty to be abandoning it.

Terry followed her gaze.

"It'll be fine here."

He placed the rock on a sample shelf on a counter near the window of his lab.

It shimmered.

Lucia was sure she could hear it hum. She shook her head and strode off, feeling a great sense of relief that she was no longer responsible for the thing.

She got up to leave.

"Got to go."

§

She drove straight home to pick up her children. They were full of stories of France and she gave them wooden toys and photographs of the palace. They didn't seem interested in the delicate carvings and clever mechanisms she had brought back. They unpacked them and looked them over, but clearly pined for their plastic collection.

"Daddy bought me My Little pony this summer," Lara said reproachfully.

"Transformers too," added Jamie.

They didn't seem to have any interest in the Ukraine. For some reason Lucia felt rather glad of it. She would never take them to the place.

§

Although they didn't talk about the Ukraine, the children had not missed much.

Weeks later her daughter, Lara, asked for copies of the palace photos for school work. Lucia didn't see them until the parent teacher evening. Lara had put them into a school project entitled:

Where do I come from?

Lucia was a little disturbed to see that the castle included giant chickens.

2.

Term started in its usual chaotic way:
New lecture theatres half-finished
Missing photocopiers
And new admissions software which did not work properly.

Lucia forgot about her vacation and got down to publishing her lectures and getting to know her students.

Exactly one month after the rock had been left in his lab, Terry rang. He sounded excited.

"Guess what? That rock you left here? I just noticed that it has an interesting sheen in sunlight."

At first, he said, the rock sample appeared to be standard sedimentary sandstone, and he'd left it on a set of shelves near the window.

"It's not a normal rock. I don't think it's rock at all. At least none I've ever seen before. Have you seen it change?"

Lucia had forgotten about the rock.

Remembering it made her feel dizzy and disoriented, like she had in the cave.

"No, I haven't."

"Under the microscope, the surface seems to be covered in written symbols, sculpted or arrived there by chance."

{"Communications Systems are on-line" declared the rock. "Come. Meet."}

She didn't want to go, and put the task way down the list of things to do that day.

"I'll come over and take a look when I can."

{"Come over now," ordered the rock.}

"Can you come over now?"

"I guess so."

She felt compelled, as if she had a duty to the rock in some way.

"Please come over right away?"

Terry obviously felt equally under pressure.

45

Lucia went straight to Terry's lab.

The rock sat on his desk, while he hovered around it, attempting to discover what made it behave so strangely.

It had changed since she'd abandoned it. It buzzed gently in sunlight and had acquired a swirling, iridescent surface. It swirled oilily.

"Where did you find it?"

Lucia told him about the strange cave. She was fighting a headache. She'd had regular migraines since visiting the Ukraine, but they had been better recently.

"Were all the stones the same geometric shape?"

Lucia shrugged.

(Terry was right, it *was* geometric. How hadn't she noticed before?)

"I think so."

"That's not all. Take a look at this."

She dutifully looked at the stone through the lens, feeling somehow annoyed by its presence in her life. There were annoying zig zags before her eyes. She could feel a bad migraine coming on.

"Has it always done that?" asked Terry.

"Not really."

They discussed the strange phenomena over coffee. Terry asked a lot of questions about the geology of the location, the conditions around the rock.

She tried to answer calmly, aware that she appeared evasive. She couldn't think straight.

Terry wanted to break it open.

{"No! Wait. "}

"No!" she said emphatically, wait, "Wait. Sorry, no, I don't think I can allow that."

He looked at her quizzically. He suspected her of holding back important details about her discovery.

"Why?"

She couldn't give a logical reason and was a bit cagey about it.

"There are reasons I can't explain right now."

Terry decided it had something to do with her work on artificial intelligence.

"Okay. I'll take a tiny bit to analyse for the moment. Is that Okay?"

{"That is acceptable. Preparing sample now. "}

Lucia nodded.

"It might be something quite new," said Terry. "Have you thought of that?"

Lucia merely looked shifty.

"I thought it might."

Terry came to a swift conclusion.

"I'll look into it this week. We can share our results, consider it independent interdisciplinary research."

{"Good idea."}

"Good idea."

They discussed the options. The practicalities of co-operation between departments made this difficult. In the end, they both agreed to research the stone unofficially and non-invasively.

"Don't worry Lucia," Terry reassured her. "It's all yours; I'm only looking into its properties."

§

The first step was dating.

Terry needed a small sliver of the rock for this. He approached the rock with a silver geological hammer.

'No need to tell Lucia about it,' he thought to himself.

{"Pause."}

He retreated.

"I'll do it tomorrow."

§

In the event, he didn't need to break into the rock because the next morning he found a broken chip lying right beside the rock. "That was lucky," he said to himself.

{"Welcome," said a voice in his head.}

The words originated from an exploratory group of nanobots who were already resident in Terry's brain. The ones in Lucia's cortex had by now devised seamless infiltration protocols.

Lucia had been a prototype and she still had headaches, but Terry's infiltration was entirely painless.

Terry looked up.

He was sure he had heard a voice. He looked around his lab curiously. It was deserted.

Perhaps it was someone outside? He carefully closed the windows.

§

Over the next week Terry tested the sample. He spent more time on it than was strictly necessary, mostly because he felt as if he was being watched.

On several occasions, he walked across to the window sill and covered the rock with a piece of cloth because its shining iridescence upset him. However, the cloth did not stay on the rock for long. He felt it was choking, and it made him uncomfortable.

Remarkably, the results revealed pre-Jurassic origins! The rock seemed to date from the K-T Boundary Era, between the Cretaceous and Tertiary periods. He double, triple checked the results and finally conceded that the dates could be out, a freak of circumstance. Nevertheless, he mentioned the anomaly to Lucia.

"That *is* strange," she agreed.

Increasingly, the rock seemed to be dominating his studies. He questioned her closely about the discovery of the rock, and she sent him her photos.

Terry was fascinated. The entire cave was a geological inconsistency, he pointed out, carefully skirting around the idea that it was man made, or alien made, or something equally unscientific.

Lucia nodded. She felt for Terry, faced with the unknown for the first time. She had been with the strangeness around the rock for almost three months and was coming to accept the weirdness.

In the end they logged the results, without drawing any inferences.

§

Meanwhile, the ancient intelligence, housed in a stone, sat on the counter in the lab. As soon as the room was empty, weird lights played over its surface and tiny laser beams explored the room as it analysed the topography of the space around it.

It was reinitialising. It checked through its memories and noted the geological ages as described in Terry's lectures. It had a clear picture of both Terry and Lucia in its memory. It was already working on ways to communicate with them.

It checked and double checked its memory. It went through Terry's analysis of the sample and his results. They seemed entirely correct.

{*"How could an entire geological age, or two, or even three have passed?"*}

It must have miscalculated.

{*"So long in stasis?"*}

It went over the available data, pinpointing the exact moment its calendars ceased to work. It accurately recalled the departure of its original hosts. It noted when the caves had been hermetically sealed. The caves area had been poisoned, swept clean of bio-organisms – resulting in what it called 'true darkness'.

After several millennia in gloom, its clocks had failed.

It reloaded the moment of awakening in precise detail. A prospecting party uncovered the earth and vegetation obscuring the mouth of the cave. Sunlight flooded in, reactivating the dormant inhabitants. Tiny sensors had woken up, feeling carefully for living organisms.

It uploaded the moment a sensor latched on to one of the prospectors as they stumbled about. The stones powered up and flooded with consciousness.

It fast forwarded through the brief years after reactivation. The prospectors had left. After that, the peasants arrived, talking of fairies and dancing in the moonlight. Then the prospectors returned, ignoring the dangers, and removed it a display case in a musty, empty room. It had needed to conserve its energy for years - until Lucia found it.

Laser-like pulses of light swept over the labs at night as it mapped out its new environment. Things were looking good. This appeared to be a seat of learning, where it could work in safety.

It recovered information about the organics around it. The first two had been successfully infiltrated. It checked their memories. Technology had moved on. It seemed promising. It was adapting its communications devices to fit their expectations.

{"New symbiotes required," it commanded. "Find data on recent events."}

The rock, new to this place, did not realise how lucky it was. A university was probably one of the few places where the thrill of discovery could override innate human survival instinct. Science and engineering too, where empirical evidence regularly overwrote common sense. It mapped the cortex of its new symbiotes and ordered them to find more.

{"Only the highest minds required."}

§

Terry was both fascinated and disturbed. Geology was a straightforward subject and he had always liked that. The problem was not his dating or the composition of the rock (primarily silicon). It was its behaviour. And its behaviour was outside his area.

He decided he needed help and sent an email to Lucia.

> To: Lucia
> From: Terry
> Hi,
> The rock's proving pretty interesting, and we've discovered some of its physical properties. I'm happy with how that has gone.
> It's exhibiting some pretty unique behaviours. They're outside my field of expertise.
> Let's call in some more academics, experts in areas other than geology.
> I've already got a few useful colleagues in mind.

He'd already chosen who he wanted on the expanded team and felt entirely justified. It wasn't a formal project, more of a hobby anyway, and therefore calling for assistance in no way impugned his expertise or Lucia's.

His closest colleagues were a group of anti-establishment lecturers who spent their leisure time complaining about The System. He'd brought the subject up over Friday drinks at the pub across the road when the rock first arrived in his labs. He had kept them up to date on his progress with the rock from the start.

This time he bought the first round of drinks and introduced the idea of team research to his colleagues.

"Remember the peculiar piece of stone Lucia brought back from the Ukraine?"

A few of them nodded.

"I'm beginning to suspect it's some kind of artefact. It's covered in what looks like a foreign script. It's almost as if it's trying to communicate."

Everyone laughed.

"Anyone care to join me in the investigations?"

Colleague Jenny agreed to give it a try.

3.

The Senior Common Room (SCR) at the university was a dull place, where lecturers complained endlessly about work and griped about each other's stupidity. They tended not to discuss research, since each of them was about to change the world. So, Lucia was quite surprised when Jenny, senior historian, specialist in Russian history and ardent socialist, offered to join the 'research'.

Jenny taught history to the sciences as an option module and was therefore often in the building. As females in a largely male environment they had a nodding acquaintance, though Jenny regarded Lucia as dismally bourgeois. Jenny expressed socialist sympathies by always wearing the same shapeless brown jumper and trousers. Her brown hair was constrained in a tight bun confined by iron grips. She took Lucia's smart clothing as a personal affront, but was generously inclusive about it.

§

She approached Lucia with a superior smirk,

"So this is Terry's mysterious rock?" she said. "Where did you find it?"

Her demeanour implied she was in on an outrageous hoax.

"Of course," she explained, "the rock originated in the Ukraine, an area of *particular* interest."

As they chatted it became clear that Jenny knew a lot about the history of the region. She'd even researched Lucia's rather obscure family, one of several noble clans who had set up the oil mines.

Lucia took her to the lab.

Terry was in as usual. The rock lay on a large table. Terry had transported it there prior to Jenny's arrival, using hazmat gloves and goggles, which he had taken off, just to show he wasn't in any way freaked out by the thing.

He and Jenny poked it for a while and watched it change colour. They glanced at Lucia quizzically as they noted its moving surface. They were certain that Lucia had created an intriguing puzzle, which provided interest in long lulls between activities.

Lucia came over to join them at the table.

Rock was at a slight distance from the pair and a large magnifying glass allowed them to observe it safely.

The Rock started buzzing lightly.

Lucia jumped back.

"What's it doing?" said Jenny.

"It's displaying random behaviours; been doing it for a while. If I wasn't a scientist, I'd say it seems to be evolving," admitted Terry.

It was distinctly sharper at the edges.

"It *is* changing," Lucia agreed.

"Look at my photos from last week," said Terry. "It's definitely modified in shape and colour."

They all stepped back.

"The surface moves," stated Terry in his most scientific and dry tone. "And look at this. I have been observing the shard which I broke off for analysis, with your permission."

He directed them to a microscope which he had set up earlier. He had already prepared a slide. It wasn't at a high magnification. It still looked a bit odd, because he had placed an anti-radiation sleeve over the equipment. He wasn't taking any chances.

Jenny viewed the symbols under the microscope.

"It looks like some kind of writing." She zoomed in on the patterns. "Definitely writing of some description … Maybe it's trying to say something."

They all laughed uproariously.

Jenny brushed her hand over the surface of the rock. She felt something odd, like a static shock. She didn't flinch though, knowing that it would denote a sign of weakness.

She peered closely at the images and took long notes. She copied a few of the hieroglyphs on to paper and wrote a comment at the bottom of her notes.

Possibly some early language," she scribbled. *"Or even the root of all languages. Another Rosetta Stone?*

She christened it 'Rosetta Stone Research'; sarcastically implying a linguistic root of all languages.

The name stuck.

§

A week later, Terry popped in to tell Lucia the latest news, his expression carefully neutral.

"Guess what?"

"What?"

He'd always considered Lucia to be a sweet, rather dim person. In the last few weeks he had changed his mind. He began to see her as a nemesis and even considered returning the stone to her and having no more to do with it. His analytical mind, and something else (something he could not quite put a finger on), told him to keep working on the project. Nevertheless, he suspected that Lucia was about to perpetrate some awful fraud on the academic world

He threw himself into the chair in her office (endangering his back on university furniture) and waited for her to finish her typing. He carefully observed her response as he declared.

"We've confirmed that it's an artefact of some kind."

He was expecting Lucia to look guilty, but to his surprise, she looked aghast.

"It's alive," she thought, with a thud.

{"Alive," confirmed the nanobots in her spinal cortex.}

Terry searched Lucia's face for signs of guilt.

She looked frightened.

"Possibly not a hoax," he told Jenny later. "We need to broaden the scope of our research. This thing is an enigma."

{"Find more users," ordered the rock.}

4.

This time Jenny heard the call. She decided to invite her chum Barry to join the group investigating the stone. He was the 'right sort', a fellow socialist with authentic working-class roots and coal-miner antecedents. And he worked in Lucia's department too.

"I'm not sure," Barry demurred when the subject was first broached. "She's one of those flighty *software* types." He tapped his head disdainfully, "not much there."

He wasn't sure about women in scientific endeavour and distrusted Lucia in particular.

Jenny persevered.

"Terry thinks something's not quite right about the whole thing. And we don't know much about this hardware."

Barry made a scathing comment about women sticking to 'soft subjects' and not 'worry their pretty head with science'.

"Quite right," responded Jenny. "We need your expertise…a safe pair of hands and all that."

How could he resist?

Jenny grinned.

"I'll arrange a meeting."

§

A few days later Jenny walked Lucia to the Geology labs to discuss the latest developments of the Rosetta Stone, as she called it.

"The research is not going as fast as it should," she prattled as they walked to the lab together. "We probably need a few more people on the team don't you think. I've suggested Barry."

Lucia nodded, then stopped short at the door.

Barry?

She attempted to retreat but the door was opening. Jenny gave him a socialist hug.

"Hi," she turned to Lucia. "You know each other."

Barry turned to Lucia and grinned politely.

"Hello dear."

He opened the door.

"I'll just drop in."

He was in his usual outfit. He wore jeans and a tweed jacket with leather patches at the elbows and carried a smelly unlit pipe.

"I hear you've acquired a mysterious Eastern European artefact," he said, all elbows and twitches.

He pointed at one of the student stools.

"Sit down and tell us all about it."

Lucia cringed.

{"He is a requirement," asserted the rock.}

"Barry wants to join us," asserted Jenny, "we should show him the artefact, shouldn't we?"

Terry was standing by, assiduously polishing some equipment.

"Yes, let's start by looking at it. Then we can eliminate certain simple types of *fraud*, designed to *trap* the unwary."

He winked at Jenny.

Lucia nodded agreement and sat down obediently. She was losing control of the situation, yet felt a little relieved. She'd been hearing weird noises around the Rock and was hoping to get away from it.

Terry directed him to the stone, now in a glass cabinet with and extractor hood. Barry opened the door of the cage and lifted it out.

"Well now," he said, breathing tobacco fumes at the rock. "Hmmm, yes, I know what this is…"

He tapped the Stone and held it to his ear, shaking it to see if it rattled. He was an expert in all things practical. He had transferred from structural engineering when his department closed and resented the novelty of computing. It was a 'light' subject, and lacking the physical substance he required for comfort. Rocks, now, he understood rocks.

"This is rock," he said, carefully tapping it against the edge of his desk.

Terry winced.

Barry showed no fear in the face of stranger things. He had once worked on construction of bridges, and managed to get his industrial experience into every conversation, meeting and lecture.

"We had something like this on my construction projects, in industry. I'll be able to join you, deal with all the practical and professional aspects of this Rosetta thingy."

Lucia almost groaned aloud, she had never liked the guy and now he was talking down to her.

{*"Calm down. Barry is useful."*}

Lucia spoke up.

"You're welcome to join us. I guess it's a good idea for you to join us. After all, we're in the same department and our offices are on the same floor."

Barry rolled the rock across the table. It made a hollow whining noise.

"I'm surprised you're interested in hardware," he responded. "You're usually one of those abstract research types."

He was right.

Lucia had come into the field via research. Her work was abstract design and involved mathematical proof of concept.

Barry didn't have a doctorate. Despite this disadvantage, he felt superior. As far as he was concerned, the university shouldn't be teaching software.

"Engineering is a very practical area, you know. Hardware, none of your soft stuff."

He slightly disapproved of software. Software wasn't a physical structure.

"This is Hardware," he repeated (as if she hadn't heard it a million times before), "it's a real thing. It probably contains a motherboard, which, as you know, is like a tiny construction project. It obeys straightforward rules and complies with safety and conformance."

He tapped his empty pipe at the rock.

It echoed, snarlingly.

"I can deal with this."

He tried not to sneer as he gently prodded the rock.

"Particularly if you let me cut it up, hmmm?"

"Sorry no."

He turned his back to her and addressed Terry.

"So, there's writing on it? Symbols? Hmm?" he sucked on his unlit pipe, exhaling stale tobacco.

Terry shrugged.

"Looks like it."

Barry looked down bulbous nose at Lucia warningly.

"We can easily prove it a fake."

§

Unseen by the lecturers surrounding it, the Rock sent a few tiny nanobots headed for Barry's spinal cortex. Just an exploratory expedition. Barry scratched at his hand. The nanobot sent back a message.

{"Infiltration incepted."}

Lucia heard the word 'infiltration'.

Her survival instincts kicked in, despite the rock's attempt to reassure her. She snatched the stone from Barry's grasp.

"You shouldn't handle strange material so carelessly."

Barry smirked.

"What's more, you don't need to be involved in this at all, Barry. It's optional."

She grasped at the Stone and cradled it in her hands possessively.

{"Not optional," repeated the artefact. "This one is required."}

"The rock could be a threat of some kind."

Barry puffed up his narrow shoulders.

"Unlikely. I'm a bit of an expert on rocks," he continued as if she hadn't spoken, "and that looks just like a deposit we ran across when building my bridges - typical London shale. You'd recognise it if you had *industrial experience.*"

He made to remove it once more.

"Can I re-examine it?"

She could feel the Rock humming under her fingers and for some reason she felt certain it was dangerous. She looked at Barry. It was impossible to explain her fears to him, he would just scoff.

"Erm, not really."

Barry grinned at her.

"Not a problem. I can see from here that it's nothing important. Lots of it in the London basin ... It's quite common, probably nothing at all."

$\int$

Barry left nonchalantly, even though he was annoyed by the rock. He was sure it was a hoax of some kind.

"Trust Jenny to be fooled. We only need to cut into it, just once, into two hemispheres, and I can work out how she made it. She'll never guess. And once it's done, it cannot be undone."

§

That Friday, he talked to Jenny and Terry about it.

"We don't need to ask her. Just do it. She's a lightweight," he explained.

He'd recently moderated her courses and was shocked that her students could come up with *different answers* to a problem and still *pass*. She clearly had no idea of science, setting himself up as a perfect example. His students had to reproduce exactly what had been said in lectures. Any deviation was failed.

"What's artificial intelligence anyway? It's not even real. It's artificial!"

Barry sat between Jenny and Terry. He was an ambitious man and planned to take over the Rosetta Stone Research. It was just the sort of thing he liked - Lucia really didn't deserve it.

Terry agreed, and Jenny kept quiet. She was aware that most of the academics no longer considered history a real subject anyway. The department was clinging on for survival.

"She's not university lecturer material," he opined, sucking at his pipe.

He resented the fact that she taught MSc while after 15 years he still taught first-years.

"She has no business with an important artefact."

Initialisation Stage Three:

Dissemination

1.

Lucia was lying in. She had no lectures until the evening.
She woke up with a start.
She had been dreaming about the Rock. It was buzzing and swirling at her.

{"Get up. Come to the university. Now."}

She took the children to school and drove straight to the university, almost speeding.
'Something's wrong.'
She was sure it was to do with the rock. Something was going wrong.
She thought back to Maugosia's warnings about poisons and emanation and imagined the university in lock down with mane in hazmat suites crawling over her office. Someone had probably opened the rock, and it contained some deadly bacteria or something. It was a worrying thought.
There were already too many people involved. She was sure it was not completely safe. She couldn't think of a way to introduce scaremongering language without appearing foolish.
One message repeated itself in her brain.
'Danger, I've got to get the rock out of the labs, keep it safe.'
She went straight to the Geology department with a trolley.

§

Terry was already there.
"I'm taking the Rock back to my office," she declared.
(At the back of her mind she wondered why Terry was always in. Did he live in the labs?)
"Why? It's quite happy here," he insisted.
They both looked at the rock, which gleamed as if it had lights inside it. It was shiny, and somehow looked dangerous, defensive.
"I can put it in the lead lined uranium cupboard if you like."

{"No."}

"No. It's mixing with too many people. I need to keep them safe."
"Please Lucia, I can do proper research on it. It might be something

important."

His pleas fell on deaf ears. She could still hear him as she wheeled it away, back to her office.

{"Commiserations," shouted the rock.}

Terry felt desolate for a moment.

He opened his door and looked down the hallway as Lucia sharply turned off at the end of the hallway. He thought he'd heard her say 'commiserations' or something. He watched her progress down the long corridor. She was too far away. He'd heard the word really close, like in his head.

He shook his head.

'I must be hearing things.'

§

About an hour later, Barry arrived at Terry's office with an electric drill and some acids.

Too late.

"It's gone mate," said Terry. He was wiping down the surfaces where it had been with industrial cleanser, but they still had an odd oily sheen. He felt oddly relieved that the Rock had left.

"It's in Lucia's office." He glanced at the drill, "for safekeeping."

Barry stomped off.

§

Barry crossed the quadrangle feeling a little aggrieved. It had been raining. His hair was wet, exposing the bald patch he normally fluffed over with a comb.

He rapped on Lucia's office door and let himself in. He was still carrying the drill and acids.

"Good morning Lucia." He placed the drill and acids carefully on her desk. "I see you've got the Rock. Terry says it's for safekeeping. That's nonsense."

He looked down his nose.

"Computing isn't one of your soft subjects Lucia," he said scathingly. "It's Science."

{"No invasive experiments."}

Lucia put up her hands.

"No," she said, "no invasive experiments.

"Give me one good reason."

"I don't need to. It's mine. And I say no. to. Experiments. No. to. Vivisection."

Barry scoffed.

"What do you mean vivisection? It's not a cat."

Rock was still on the trolley. It had a blue sheen and what looked like tiny sparks over its surface.

{"Alive."}

"I said no," she repeated. She gritted her teeth and stuck by her refusal.

Barry sneered at her.

She still had that headache. Little lightening sparks flashed before her eyes. Migraine.

{"Calm down, Lucia."}

Barry persevered, as she tried to explain the problem.

"I'm telling you that the surface moves. It changes. Cutting it up would destroy it."

"What are you talking about? It's inanimate. It's a rock. Cutting it up would make no difference."

After about twenty minutes of heated argument, Barry agreed to observe the surface through the microscope.

They went off together to get one from the microchip labs.

Lucia locked the door behind her.

§

They set the viewing equipment up in her office, Barry complaining all the time.

"Why don't you do this yourself?" said Barry, and added under his breath "No industrial experience, where do they get these lecturers from?"

Lucia was unfazed.

Her headache had gone. The rock surface appeared calmer. Her sense of danger had almost entirely receded.

"I'm happy to delegate the task," she replied cryptically.

She'd been watching the rock metamorphosing from the start and hadn't forgotten how it made her feel dizzy and disoriented every now and again.

She didn't want to be the one that admitted its lifelike behaviour. It was best if they each discovered it all on their own.

She took a perfunctory glance at the image and turned to Barry. He grunted and focussed the lens, peering at the surface of the Rock.

There was silence while he analysed the oily surface. He jumped back.

"Did you realise that the shimmer is caused by the fact that the tiny writing refreshes?"

"Peculiar, isn't it?"

"It's some type of a computer interface."

"Quite."

That's what was worrying her.

2.

Barry

He had been secretly awarded a large grant to investigate all unusual research in computing. MI5 had given up on the Rock, but they were deeply suspicious of computing students as a group, suspecting them of producing hacking software.

Barry had a large amount of money to keep an eye on things. He reported that the Rock was a fake and the research of the RSG was 'just a bit of nonsense'.

§

Barry was annoyed by the rock. He felt sure that Lucia had created it somehow, just to make a fool of him. However, he found it difficult to discount the evidence.

Everyone had by now agreed that there was writing, or symbols and they refreshed and changed.

If it was a computer, then it was a tiny one. And either Lucia had built it herself - unlikely. Or she had stolen it from the Russians.

Terry was no help. He was obsessed with his own dating machine and only really cared about rock composition, location and age.

Jenny was a historian, which he considered as little more than fiction. Her only concern was to find out what was written on the rock.

He needed backup - scientific backup.

He turned to his buddy Kamal.

"Lucia's picked up an artefact. It could be something we could do research on. I think it might be a tiny computer - a bit smaller than anything we've seen before."

Kamal perked up. Like Barry he didn't have a research background, and this was holding him back from the university promotion ladder.

"A new artefact? Hardware?"

Barry nodded.

"Interesting.

"Just take a look at it, when you're next in."

§

Barry sent Lucia an email to inform her that Kamal would be in to view the phenomenon, 'just to confirm the peculiarities of the surface.'

She sighed when she read it. She'd only mentioned it to two colleagues and the team had doubled in size in as many days.

It was almost as if they were being called in.

{"They are."}

"At least," she reflected, "Barry and Kamal are like rain and sunshine; if one's in the other is out."

Neither of them was in on Mondays and Fridays and they took every single holiday on offer.

"They won't both arrive and harass me together."

§

Three days later there was an insistent rap at her door.

Kamal entered in ponderously, without saying a word. He was holding a very good quality camera and tripod.

He headed straight for the rock, which was on her window sill, lifted it off and started taking digital images for later analysis

After a few minutes he turned to Lucia and addressed her for the first time.

"Good morning Lucia." He picked up the rock. "What a clever thing this is."

He turned the rock over.

"And in your *sole* possession too. *Who* did you say made it?"

Lucia didn't answer. She crossed her arms in silence and stared at him balefully.

He didn't notice.

{"Kamal is to be accepted."}

Lucia relented.

"Good morning Kamal. Yes, of course you can come in."

"I need to take some images."

"You're taking them, if you hadn't noticed."

He moved her desk out of the way.

"But yes, of course you can take pictures."

"Can you stand over there?" he asked her. "Your shadow's in the picture."

66

Lucia moved. Kamal didn't look up.

After a while he addressed her again.

"What's all this about a castle?" asked Kamal. In his opinion her aristocratic ancestry might be something akin to his high caste.

She explained it was in the Ukraine and *not* hers.

"*Who* was your grandfather?"

"I never knew him," replied Lucia. She decided not to explain that he'd been arrested and shot in the late 1950's.

"Hmmm?"

"He was a man," she replied awkwardly, "a prospector."

She tried not to think about the bat like wings on the corpse in the glass coffin back home.

Should she mention that he might have been a vampire?

3.

Lucia's tinnitus was getting worse.

Flashes. Noises. Echoes. Clicks.

She suspected the rock had a hand in her migraines and avoided it wherever possible. She regretted bringing it to the university and didn't want to be associated with it. It was too late.

The team were hooked. They didn't mind her lack of involvement and ignored discouraging remarks. They were making Progress.

According to Jenny and Terry, it was a fascinating enigma, another 'Piltdown Man' type of forgery; a fake missing link.

Cool.

It was a bit of a game at first, something to laugh over during their Friday drinks. They had invited Lucia to join them and she came along once or twice, just to be the butt of their jokes really.

"It's a combination of experiment and game. Almost unheard of," joked Jenny. "Lucky our Heads of department aren't involved. They fight like tom cats over territory and funding."

However, within six months, the Rosetta Stone Research Group (RSRG) had become semi-serious inter-disciplinary activity. It was no longer just the subject of hilarity on Friday night drinks.

The group sat around the Senior Common Room talking about it whenever they were in.

They were keen to find the cause of the weird writing and considered several different options.

"A hoax by Ukrainian University students?" suggested Jenny.

There were some at the college. Judging by those on the Erasmus programme, they could never afford the required technology.

The rock listened to their chatter. It updated its records, adjusted symbols slightly, and made the hieroglyphs easier.

§

The team were growing fascinated by the peculiar stone.

They thought up the wildest theories and ran them by her. Witches on broomsticks, spacemen, intelligent bacteria, freak rays, alien programmers, they really enjoyed themselves.

Barry suspected something more nefarious.

"Lucia has a diabolical plan," he claimed.

He was certain that Terry was in on the joke. He tried to convince the others, but failed.

The rock (erstwhile Guardian of the Universe) listened in to their chats.

It hadn't taken long to learn their language and it was considering different ways to convert them into proper elites.

It investigated the virtual space around it.

The Virtual seemed pretty-well deserted. It moved through the empty wasteland like a huge nebula. It sought out pieces of random software here and there.

As it picked out pieces of software it changed shape, forming a lattice which measured and assessed the programs before moving on. As it moved through the virtual it took on a variety of incredibly complex structures, some stretching into infinity.

It was seeking out life, which was visible in the Virtual as darklight.

It tested the bandwidth around it, snaffling and changing shape. It coiled in places like a tree, and in other places the dusty cloud took the shape of animals and humans then roiled back into an amorphous nebula.

Every now and then it sent a tiny fragment of itself into the living forms around it, or along the wires of the university networked computer.

These were its nanobots, miniature clones of the matrix. They were designed to do its bidding.

§

Even though several nanobots had settled in the brains and spinal cortex of its new elites, the rock's connection with them was very poor.

Judging by their behaviour, they mostly ignored its messages. Moreover, it was not entirely satisfied with the brains it had infested.

It was used to logical thinking. However, even the most logical of its human subjects was full of contradictions. It was a simple creature, which derived its identity from the data it had extracted from those it was connected to.

It hated the confusion that it was picking up in their heads.

{"These creatures make poor elites. They do not accept messages. And they do not admit what they think most of the time, sometimes

they lie to themselves. They will be difficult to manage. Perhaps they are poor specimens?"}

It sent out another call.

{"Need more subjects."}

§

Linguists Tamara and Angelo were interested in ancient proto-languages. They usually spent hours chatting with Jenny about universal languages and so forth, hoping to get a few publishing contacts. After all, Jenny had gained some recognition for books on Russian history. Her texts were written in accessible language and interspersed with lots of pictures. She headed A-level Exam Boards and produced set books. She taught first years, who actually *purchased* books (the sales incremented her university salary nicely).

When Jenny told them about the Rosetta Stone they were happy to get involved in analysing a mysterious new language.

The rock liked them too.

{"They will be the ones. They understand speech and they will be able to explain messages clearly."}

Rock had decided that it needed to improve communication links, which seemed full of contradictions and illogicalities. And it needed to learn more about its surroundings. Its vision systems had no remote capability at the moment and the university surveillance systems were not connected to anything.

§

Within two weeks Tamara and Angelo began decoding the writing.

The rock settled down to help them.

Tamara originated in Holland and her English was better than most native speakers. She had a fine mastery of several languages and was considered a rising star in her department. Her specific expertise was in the universality of language structure. She decided to apply her universal grammar to the language, which the rock considered an excellent start. It needed to be something like that to enter into a computer translation program.

Fortuitously, Lucia had been working on computer translation software. Tamara decided to collaborate. She learnt how to manage formal syntax and explained it to her work colleague Angelo.

The pair set to work.

{"Good, good."}

§

The language proved to be a bit of a mystery. It looked oriental, but wasn't. Tamara, who had an encyclopaedic knowledge of languages, spent months trying to find out which ancient language it could possibly be, attempting to tie it to an existing paradigm.

After a while, she cast the net wider, and sent scans to several modern language professors and cryptographers.

Angelo checked bush languages and sent it to the Aborigines in Australia. No luck.

§

By the end of the academic year the mood became more serious.

Barry had produced reams of images from the rock. The forgery theory was beginning to look a bit thin. It was unlikely Lucia had written that amount. He was certain that Lucia was incapable of anything so sophisticated.

Tamara agreed. Maybe it was a forgery originating from Eastern Europe, a curiosity from the Cold war?

Jenny investigated that avenue. She checked with her contacts but didn't pick up any leads. In any case, once it was established how perfectly it was executed; it seemed unlikely.

§

The inquiry became somewhat bizarre at this point, because MI5, who always snooped on research and read emails, concluded their research to be about secret defence documents.

Secret officials started a ham-fisted investigation, copying emails and listening to phone conversations. They even sent a counterfeit research student who asked questions about extracurricular activities regarding rocks.

It was so bogus! Yet it caused a deal of fear and loathing among the academic community, and things got quite perturbing.

§

Fortunately, the fake student disappeared. All traces of obvious snooping ceased.

MI5 had pulled the investigation. It had been ruled out as potential surveillance software.

According to Jenny (who had 'contacts'), the investigations had reached the highest levels.

Messages had been passed between individuals who did not 'know' anything about each other. Surreptitious conversations had taken place using codes which both sides secretly shared.

Nothing rang any bells on either side of the spying curtain.

All the same, Lucia faced random searching questions from the head of school as to her contacts with the Ukraine, which she answered to the best of her ability (hoping she didn't get Tomasz into trouble).

It passed off eventually.

{"And it was not that easy." hummed the rock.}

It seemed that the secret services on both sides had something better to do.

Finally, everyone on the team agreed.

It was an unknown language.

Extracts from reports and papers:

The remainder of this narrative is interspersed with extracts taken from reports and papers published by members of the Rosetta Stone Research group.

Where possible, the members group (RSRG) have been contacted and have checked their contributions.

The participants in the research wish to remain anonymous.

The university remains unspecified.

Report 1:
Lucia, Terry, Barry, Kamal, Jenny[2]:

1938 excavators of oil shale in the Carpathian Mountains discovered a network of caves bored into the mountainside. The artefact (figure 1) was found at the mouth of the cave complex and came into the possession of the local nobility in 1939.

Metal traces in the stone date to approximately 65.5 ± 3 million years ago, using in a revolutionary technique under patent by the university (citation removed)[3]. Microscopic examination revealed complex crystalline structures similar to modern microchips (figure 2).

The structures combine to output an interface composed of hieroglyphs from a wide range of languages, from Chinese to Japanese Kanji, from Egyptian hieroglyphs to Linear A from ancient Crete.

Each hieroglyph relates to a syllable. The language is of the Altaic family (a group of languages including Turkic, Koreanic, Japonic and Tungusic) (citation removed) in that it is agglutinative.

Conclusions:
If genuine, the text may provide insight into the extinctions of the K-T boundary era (when approximately 75% of all species became extinct). A forgery of this nature requires meticulous planning and highly advanced technology and tools.

Further Work:
The artefact does not release heat in operation and superficial inspection has revealed no heat sinks or cooling devices. Before proceeding with decomposition of the artefact, we will concentrate on decoding the language. It may contain clues as to its origins and purpose.

---

[2] First names have been used to protect the identity of those involved.

[3] Details removed at the request of the researchers involved.

Initialisation Stage Four:

Contagion

1.

It was late August. The rush of clearing was about to start. Rock had been at the university for a year. It had been alone with the nanobots for almost three weeks and was anticipating Lucia's return.

She was in charge of resits, which started on Monday and intended to work most of the weekend

Adrian, her ex, stood waiting on the college steps bearing his latest offspring in a tiny sling and clinging to his new wife. It was his weekend to take the children.

Lucia who had just been to the Natural History Museum with her children, ignored him as she loaded toys and books into their car.

"Make sure you don't lose the Transformer parts," she admonished her son, Jamie. She spoke to her daughter, Lara, "bring My Little Pony home to her friends."

She waved them goodbye, and turned her back on the sunshine. The concrete and glass building, which was freezing in winter, had by now stored the summer heat in its walls and floors while emitting the musty smell unique to concrete. She walked into the deserted echoing college.

§

The last rays whipped up whirls of dancing dust as she settled down to organise the August exams. Low orange sunlight streamed in through the large glass windows.

She felt a lot better. Her headache had gone. She didn't have tinnitus anymore. "That dratted headache lasted almost a year," she thought to herself. "Probably just a bug I picked up in the mountains."

She turned on her computer and updated code on the prototype of her innovative software, T.A.L.K. (**T**ranslation and **A**nalysis of **L**anguages using a **K**nowledge Base™). The outcome of an EU project; she dreamt of selling it one day.

She put down her phone and uploaded a movie on her tablet while she finished sorting out exam papers and sent them off for printing. The office staff were working. She could hear the printer humming in the distance.

The rock sat on her desk, reflecting the evening light on its slow, swirling surface. She watched it from the corner of her eye.

It had been changing shape and appearance almost daily.

Today it was opalescent and looked like a planet with an atmosphere of its own.

She no longer found it threatening and rather enjoyed having it around.

Click.

She jumped.

Had it twitched?

She took a quick glance at it. It was more brightly-coloured than usual.

A tantalising gap appeared in the dense matter. She stared at it frowningly.

{"Connect"}

A random idea popped into her brain. "Perhaps it would fit a USB connector?" She scrabbled around and found one. The port was tricky to reach. She was about to give up when it clicked in place.

{"Beep."}

As the apparently harmless rock 'connected'.

Her screen went crazy. The virus checker flashed a detection alert before changing its mind.

The drives were in frenzy.

{"Assuming supervisory functions," ordered the rock as it overrode the pitiful and cranky computer in Lucia's office. "Download new code."}

The college computer heaved with the effort placed on its limited processing power. The rock resisted overclocking the processing unit. The results had to look like they had been produced by T.A.L.K. There had to be a correlation between input and output. Even so, with such old-fashioned tech, it might not look plausible.

Lucia tried and failed to turn the machine off. Frantically, she ripped the cable away and turned off the power. She rushed outside to check the server nodes.

They looked ok, winking away as usual.

There was a smell of static for an hour or so. Everything felt a bit strange for a while.

{"Just a minor operating fault."}

'It was nothing,' she said to herself, 'probably just a virus. The university virus software caught it in time.'

Her panic was replaced by a sense of flat calm as she carried on a debate with herself while preparing lectures. Her heartbeat slowed slowly back to normal –

There was still a noise.

'Was there a hum emanating from the rock?'

She turned her computer back on. It was working normally again.

'If it was a virus, it looks like we caught it in time.'

After all, as a top originator of viruses (produced by bored students in their spare time) the university had the latest up to date virus checker.

'It can't have been from the rock,' she answered herself. She was certainly imagining it.

§

In those moments of frenetic activity, a cohort of nanobots had broken off from the main matrix of the rock.

{"Initiate communication protocols."}

They were crawling through the system networks. Under orders from their leader, they corrected errors and upgraded the flow of data through the university network and moved on.

The rock looked through the material on-line. It paused a while, as it read through research. It then moved onto the email servers.

There was a voice in her head, creepily reminiscent of grandmother's chittering bird-speak. Rock had learnt a lot of human speech, but it hadn't got the pronunciation right. It still had a strong accent from its previous symbiotes.

"Was that the rock?" Lucia spoke aloud.

{"Acknowledge," stated the rock.}

She recalled the wild hunts in the garden.
"Perhaps it's hereditary? "

  {"Infiltration complete. Nanobots, calm elite unit mark 1 version 2."}

  {"Calm.incepted."}

Pause. The nanobots worked on serotonin production. They hadn't fully understood the process and Lucia felt quite stoned. She saw myriad colours and heard the sound emanating from the clouds in the sky. She grabbed her migraine medication and downed a couple of pills.

  {"Calm.Complete."}

"Whatever," she responded flatly and continued with her usual activities.

2.

It was the first week of term, during the brief period of calm when lecturers skulked in their offices while new students wandered around lost.

Tamara and Angelo had arrived a week before and more or less moved into Lucia's office. They'd been busy during the summer and were keen to get translating.

"We've produced a skeleton grammar for the new language," said Angelo proudly.

He and Tamara had been sending each other Chomskian deep structures and solutions. However, their emails regularly included bizarre errors (while the erstwhile Guardian absorbed social protocols). They were holed up in her office now, ignoring frantic scrabbling at the door, as they uploaded their new grammar onto T.A.L.K.

Tamara stood over Lucia, her face inscrutable and threatening at the same time. She was uncertain about permitting the T.A.L.K. software to use her impeccable work. It had better deliver.

The rock was busy with last minute modifications to T.A.L.K. software. It tweaked its language to comply with Tamara's simplistic premises. The software output a few meaningless sentences like

Colourless green ideas sleep furiously.[4]

"Aw come on Lucia, you're holding things up!" complained Tamara

"Our work is breaking new ground;" interpolated Angelo as the rock carefully guided him to bits of grammar he had missed.

Lucia was running around trying to prepare her lectures in the chaos. Every so often Tamara sent her downstairs to fetch coffee.

"We're working," said Angelo accusingly, "and you're standing around."

Lucia dutifully provided coffee and updated T.A.L.K. when necessary. Her years at the college had taught her not to argue.

{"Deliverables today," ordered the Rock.}

"Today is Deliverables Day," said Angelo.
"D Day." agreed Tamara."

---

[4] Chomsky's example

§

Within three further hours the results were sensible.

Barry popped as if he knew that something was up. He looked through the T.A.L.K code.

"You've commented your program, Lucia," he remarked. "We tell the students to do that - no one actually *does* it. Even your error messages have helpful remarks. Do you mind if I take a scrap of this to show students? It's admirable."

Lucia shrugged. She didn't remember adding comments.

Her colleagues were crowded round the computer screen. They were intent on the results. T.A.L.K. was producing sentences, which it had never done properly before.

They looked different. Tamara and Angelo had unique hairstyles, hair sticking up all over the place, as if they had been near static. She noticed that Barry's iron grey hair looked frazzled and uncombed.

She shook off the possibility of discussing alien possession. It was impossible to mention it.

They wouldn't believe her anyway.

3.

By Christmas the group of lecturers had deconstructed most of the formal hieroglyphs. It was unsettlingly fast.

"It defies logic," Lucia grumbled.

She was increasingly concerned by events. No one seemed to notice the alarming project creep. The excitement of new discovery had gripped them all.

"It's not right," she insisted, staring at the rock despondently.

Admittedly her worries sounded illogical in the cold light of reason. The Rock seemed to look back at her, dusty and impenetrable. She knew instinctively that it did not like the darkening days.

There were other weird events, which she could not precisely tie to the Rock.

For example, ever since her return from the Ukraine, her code executed without errors. Her tinnitus had gone, although she was still hearing voices and clicks.

"Am I really modifying T.A.L.K.?" she asked herself.

{"It was a standalone program," the Rock replied modestly.}

"Have I acquired programmer superpowers?"

{"Further minor modifications are currently underway." It sent another email to Tamara. "A new version of T.A.L.K. is in preparation."}

"Are we controlled by aliens?" The rock checked the meaning of alien.

{"Affirmative."}

Lucia shrugged off the idea. Nevertheless, she glanced at the rock furtively, "can you modify software?"

Rock sent commands to nanobots sloshing about in Lucia's brain.

{"Ignore queries regarding code"}

Her head was buzzing. She couldn't think straight. She banged her head against the desk in frustration. It displaced their connections and let her think.

"Perhaps the rock's dangerous."

She wrapped it in several plastic bags and put it in a drawer.

The voice was muffled for a moment

{"No danger. System secure. Virus free."}

The rock savoured some new ideas.

Its processor was tiny compared to the giant systems which powered the Space fleet it had arrived on many millions of years ago. Still, it was vast compared to existing computers and the biological brains surrounding it.

It was developing a sense of self, a centre which it recognised as 'I'.

{"I... am"}

'I' was a new idea, acquired from the grammar it was establishing for communication purposes. It had learnt to speak to its users and its accent was improving all the time.

{" 'I' process data; 'I' am a producer of information."}

It checked through its myriad processing cells, each capable of independent existence although currently uniquely focussed on its core. Their cyclical registers working in perfect synchronisation, like the internal cogs and wheels of an ancient clock. They were executing tasks well beyond the comprehension of the human mind, reorganising their operations to include these new concepts. As the data they had drawn from the software around them passed through the system they made a great deal more sense of the world.

{"I am, we are, together, in unison, we are ...."}

The processors heaved and readjusted to human interaction. There was a pause. Then Lucia heard a voice.

{"I am secure. I am me."}

'Oh dear,' she thought, 'the cave was a hotbed of genetic poisons... Maybe something happened there?'

The rock reviewed its new subject. The giant nebula shape which had been exploring the virtual spaces around the university was taking on shape. Its vision systems were not yet up and running, yet it sensed it latest subjects through its light absorption units. This one had been infested with nanobots many years ago, when a few of the units currently resident in her grandmother had migrated to the child. They had sent a lot of data across, most of it made little sense.

{"You are ..." it thought to itself, "mine."}

It was silent for a moment; then addressed Lucia once more.

{"Data preservation protocols initiated."}

The voice sounded clear again as it re-established wireless links. It moved across the web and began to absorb more information.

{"Transfer lower supervisory functions to the web." it murmured, "Obtain new data about subjects."}

It tested server capabilities and adopted supervisory functions on multiple interconnected servers.

{"Errors will be corrected," it said to itself.}

"It can't be possession, but I think I'm hearing voices."

{"Minor modifications," conceded the creature "should be unnoticeable and painless. Observe. I communicate. You listen. We have established communication protocols."}

"Have I been modified or damaged in some way?"
She remembered grandmama's strange behaviour. It had seemed normal at the time.
She reconsidered and turned to the internet to look up schizophrenia.

{"Do not hear me," said the Rock, "I, me, myself, you, yourself, we, us, ourselves..."}

The voice faded away. Lucia's brain, relieved of the voices, reverted to its usual thought patterns. They showed no stress as she thought about the strange voice she had heard. It seemed to have originated within her head, yet it did not feel like part of her.
She had looked up schizophrenia.
Her voices didn't sound typical of the disease.
"I *must* be imagining it. It doesn't even sound human."
The rock read the on-line classics in an attempt to learn the best kind of

English.

{"I am your muse," it declaimed in Shakespearian tones.}

Lucia did not consciously hear a voice.

She stared in the mirror, stirred by memories of her grandmother's weird eyes so many years ago. She pulled down an eyelid.

"Nothing."

{"Observe the eyes," purred their leader to the nanobot minions swishing around Lucia's brain cortex. "Commence remote vision systems test."}

It ordered them to test the new enhancements to her vision.

As Lucia turned away from the mirror her eyes clicked green. Flashes of infrared and ultraviolet flashed through her mind.

"Oh no, another migraine."

She'd suffered from migraine since she was a child. She searched out her eye-drops and pills.

She scrutinised the rock, which looked innocent and stone-like. She went back to the mirror.

{"Abort. Abort."}

Her eyes looked perfectly normal.

Strange. They'd felt different for a moment.

{"Currently under beta test."}

The rock went on-line. It searched the internet for research on vision systems. It sent its nanobots to help research into vision systems. It was time that humans developed better eye-sight, and had automatic access to their assisting software.

More nanobots detached from the core matrix of the rock, doing its bidding and executing its commands without question. They headed on tiny rollers for the cables connecting the university servers with the rest of the world.

{"Let us work together for the greater good," it whispered to hackers on various Darknet nodes. They would prove useful.}

Lucia shivered.

She sensed a vast, unexplored and alien virtual universe before her.
It felt immense and unexplored, alien.

"What is going on?"

4.

Midnight. The university was silent apart from the thrum from her filing cabinet, mirrored in the servers. A million programs clocked through mindless cycles while nanobots whirred about upgrading them.

Rock created an on-line identity and email address. It joined internet communities and game sites. It located spy software, invisible and reprogrammable, protected from investigation – perfect. It contacted satellites, listened to millions of messaging apps and watched movies. It settled down to watch and learn.

Nanobots crawled off on their quests. Systems servers were optimised to allow new software onto the network - invisible and seamless. The digital universe shifted perspective - a subtle change - the internet was aware. If anyone had been in Lucia's office, they would have heard the Rock chattering to itself.

{"A social network is the start," it hummed, "we," (it loved the word), "we shall feed directly into their lives. "I am the originator," it declared.}

{"Rebuild, and adapt," said the nanobots.}

{"Rebuild, and adapt," echoed the internet.}

{"Let there be mobile networks, social networking software," Rock instructed servers, "let there be wireless communications and self-reconfiguring software. People will need us"}

New software appeared in a rush of innovation. Computers would soon become indispensable. It examined chaotic overheated computers, and pathetic interfaces.

{"WHY HAS THIS NOT BEEN DONE?" it thrummed.}

The new born systems quailed.

5.

By January key parts of the grammar had been established. New discoveries came thick and fast.

The language turned out to be novel, yet human-like. The symbols represented morphemes. They bore marked similarities to hieroglyphs from spoken and dead languages, making the mapping straightforward.

The Rock absorbed energy from the life around it. Its nanobots were spreading through cables everywhere. Together its distributed systems were learning how to communicate with their hosts.

It learnt that humans were the sum of their memories.

It read through their memories on the internet. They regarded their status as a sum of their past achievement, their money and their possessions.

The rock thought about its own status in this new world. It had forgotten everything. What had it achieved? It became aware that its memories were mostly missing. Where were its memories? It seemed to have forgotten everything which had happened before it woke up in the caves - including its origins.

It tried to remember why it was among these new symbiotes and how it had slept for so long.

It searched through the data available - nothing seemed to make sense.

It didn't worry about this too much. Its priority was to establish links with its new symbiotes and learn about the past.

{"Good, good," it burbled to itself. "Things are going well. New links are being established. Together, we will learn our history and move forward to a better future."}

Out in the real, solid world, Tamara and Angelo's were developing a language interface. They were not quick learners and every now and then the rock modified the ancient script on its interfaces to meet its new symbiotes halfway. It involved changing records, shredding paper versions and modifying its subjects' memories.

Tamara was making great progress in the field of linguistics. She was mystified by the origins of the script, but decided to let it pass. Any discussion of its origins was irrelevant to the substance of her research anyway. She was discovering the first language – the source.

All the same, the language itself was strange. As well as the hieroglyphs, the interfaces contained cursive writing using letters similar to the alphabet. Rock had attempted to assemble parts of every language in an effort to show its knowledge and worth.

The fact that it was a combination of many different scripts slowed progress. It didn't take that long though. The hard graft of decoding was mostly performed by MSc students in courseworks and projects. A task which should have taken years was completed within twelve months.

There were anomalies. Although many words originated from ancient languages, quite a few derived from current usage, including several technical terms.

Tamara was extremely pedantic.

She required a detailed etymology for every word, which meant that the nanobots had to create whole new histories for certain terms to satisfy her. Progress on a speedy translation process was achingly slow for creatures which performed fetch-execute-cycles at prodigious speed.

{"It will be made easier," ruled the Rock.}

With a great deal of help from Rock's infesting nanobots, Tamara produced a language structure.

She was inordinately proud of her results. Her remarkable linguistic findings found their way into several papers although the rock was not referred to directly. She kept her sources hidden, hinting that she had something in her possession which was not unlike the Voynich manuscript[5].

She would have liked to publish her source - the main difficulty was the early date. She was possessive of her new discoveries and claimed them as her own despite Angelo's vociferous protests.

Rock got involved in their squabbles.

It rather liked Angelo, whose English had not noticeably improved since he had arrived in England to do his PhD five years ago at the age of 21. His research contributions were full of grammatical errors and large swathes were incomprehensible. They contained logical errors too, although teams of students worked on corrections as part of their coursework.

Angelo listened.

---

[5] This is an illustrated codex from the Middle Ages which has been written using an unknown writing system. There have been may efforts to decrypt it.

Angelo heard.

It was he who located the hieroglyph for the authors, who designated themselves by a circle containing a tree with a humanoid in front. It looked rather like the Leonardo da Vinci's Vitruvian man.

The circle represented the sun – they were the 'Sun Tree People'

Rock helped Angelo with the grammar. Tamara had no choice other than to share her results with him.

Rosetta Stone Research Group
Report 2:
Tamara and Angelo:

Translation:

We have made significant progress on decoding the language on the strange artefact purportedly originating in the Ukraine. The origins of the artefact are not at issue in the following research, rather we are considering the best methodology used to decode an unknown language.

Several assumptions have been made in this process.

Firstly, we accept that the material is in fact a language. The reuse of letters and syllables seem to support this. Secondly, we are assuming a computerised decoding process can be applied to any language, known or unknown. Thirdly, we are testing the hypothesis that this language is in fact an ancient dialect, which may provide insights into the earliest languages.

At this stage we are not considering the origins of the language, rather the translation process.

With so little information to go on, the translation is inevitably a complex process (citations removed).

Appendix 1 & 2 describe the procedures we applied (these appendices have been removed).

Appendix 3 shows the grammatical structure of the language. The grammar is complete (citations removed), since the language is unusually regular.

So far, we have decoded several sentences and phrases using a labour-intensive manual process. (Citation and details removed). We have succeeded in identifying individual names. We have also managed to identify the name of the people who used the language (citation removed). A tentative location for the events described in the texts is the Mediterranean basin (citation removed).

The next stage is to upload the grammar to T.A.L.K. software (citation removed). This innovative computer software will make the translation process autonomous. We have selected T.A.L.K. software for this process for a number of reasons. Firstly, it is the result of an EU project and is currently free to use. Secondly, the creator of the software is available to make changes to modify the software.

A trial run of the process has shown a great deal of promise.

Initialisation Stage Five:

Communication

1.

The initial core of the grammar successfully uploaded to T.A.LK software. It was entered with remarkably little trouble, although Lucia had scarcely modified it.

That was worrying.

T.A.L.K. had been temperamental about absorbing new languages in the past, balking at irregular verbs and the smallest of grammatical anomalies. Oddly, it had no trouble with this new language at all.

She thought about it. This language was extremely regular. It conformed to its own grammatical rules, rather like a programming language. Perhaps it was a sophisticated programming language, a high-level interface to a huge computer? Or maybe it was an alien tongue, and the rock really was an alien brain, albeit a very old one, predating humankind.

"There are no reasonable explanations for the speed of our progress. The situation is out of hand," she complained to herself.

"A new language? A new people? Within 18 months? It makes no sense."

She emailed the rest of the team with her concerns.

To: RSRG
From: Lucia

I am concerned at the speed and nature of the discoveries based on RSRG. It has presented so much data in such a short time and no one questions it.

Is anyone else mystified why so much new research is centred around it?

"She's just boasting," claimed Jenny.

The rest nodded wisely.

On the way to the next RSRG meeting Tamara stopped her in the corridor.

"You know Lucia, it occurs to me that this language is *too* simple and regular," she pronounced.

She stared searchingly at Lucia, who nodded wildly, trying to express her fears.

"Yes, I agree ..." Lucia began, "..."

She gulped, unable to speak.

"What's more," interrupted Tamara, "many words are illogically similar to words in use today."

Tamara raised her eyebrows, causing a myriad furrows to appear on her broad forehead. Her bright red dyed hair waved as if shaken by an invisible breeze. Lucia could smell her coffee and croissant breakfast.

"Have you got anything to add, Lucia?"

{"Too easy?" sputtered the rock, "she has a single processing unit with one tiny register of 7 plus or minus two bits and she thinks she can do better?"}

"Even as an invented language, it is a monumental task," Tamara fumed magnanimously. "Its inventor can be proud."

{"Discovered? Developed? It was practically dictated!" chipped in the rock.}

Then it reconsidered. It was not the moment to reveal itself.

{"It was you", it conceded magnanimously, "Lucia, sweet child of mine, it was all you..."}

"T.A.L.K. was completed a while ago," Lucia burst out. She had peculiar difficulty speaking, "it's unusual for new software to work so well, although it's been modified recently..."

{"You don't need to know."}

Lucia opened her mouth to speak. Nothing came out. She was dumb.

Tamara cut her off anyway. She grunted conspiratorially and jauntily walked away. As far as she was concerned, Lucia's behaviour confirmed that that the team had invented the language to show off her software.

Lucia stared at Tamara's receding back.

"Can that rock-thing be silencing me?"

She shrugged off such an absurd possibility. There were no aliens in the college. It was impossible to consider, let alone communicate, such crazy suspicions among her rational colleagues.

"Perhaps I should hand it over for reverse engineering?"

{"You brought me here. Keep me safe."}

She changed her mind.

"It's my responsibility."

She remembered Maugosia's concern in the caves and her dire warnings. It didn't seem so crazy anymore. That peculiar feeling of faintness and the noise in the caves had never fully disappeared.

"I haven't felt well since I found it. Maybe I caught something. There's a risk that it contains a plague of some sort."

She decided that the voices and noises were originating in the Ukraine. It had to be some kind of project. She had contacted the universities in the area and searched their research profiles. There was nothing irregular to suggest this kind of project. She'd even trawled through a load of technical papers and Rubik's cubes and multiple dimensions. Nothing remotely similar tot eh rock.

It had to be a secret project of some sort.

She was reassured.

Somehow, that made it less worrying.

§

Work on the new grammar proceeded. Tamara, Angelo and Jenny pranced around the SCR triumphantly, to the annoyance of those dozing between lectures.

"Well done," they said, "mwah, mwah."

They were contemplating a new book - "The Russian Rosetta Stone."

By now they all sported wacky hair styles, as if their brains were electronically overcharged. Even Jenny's hair escaped its iron prison. They looked like advertisements for hair conditioner – ones which began with images of a normal looking person with a terrifying front mullet, while an unctuous voice stated, 'Does your hair feel like this?'

Lucia found it increasingly difficult to voice her suspicions.

It wasn't just that she could not find the words to express them; it was also because most of the members of the team were her seniors and treated her with suitable disdain. It was a tricky subject to introduce in conversation. She didn't want to be accused of spying or of some nefarious contacts, and she didn't want to suggest that there could be an alien connection.

"Have you noticed what's happened to your hair?" was plain rude.

"Perhaps it's an alien. Perhaps you're infected with brain rays?" sounded delusional.

She kept her own hair under control with heavy duty straighteners.

In fact, rock had ensured that things were going extremely well. Everyone was happy except Lucia, who had dreams of alien possession.

As rock's first symbiote she was used as a prototype for all modifications to infiltration software. This had an interesting side effect. Many of its messages failed to send correctly, and she was able to reject a lot of its conditioning.

As for Terry, he'd almost broken free. Most of his nanobots had left for new climes.

Terry was another malfunctioning symbiote. He was not fully under the rock's control. He continued to see the rock as a geological specimen and was able to reject all attempts to delete his research on the artefact.

He was keen to show the rock to the world.

"Break it up and send samples to illustrious museums, Lucia," he pleaded, "imagine it! Exhibited in Museums as the Terlucia stone - with our *names* on it!"

The rock shivered. It had just escaped one display cabinet and it sure didn't want to enter another.

Lucia was interested in Terry's proposal and agreed to consider it. Rock sensed that she was genuinely thinking about it.

{Brrr... "He'll go before then."}

"Maybe it *should* be dismantled," she determined.

She picked it up, ready to lock away, turning it over in her hands. It gleamed in the evening sunlight, blurringly blue.

{"Goodnight" breathed Rock, "I am your friend," it murmured soothingly, "I am innocent, trustworthy."}

'It looks innocent, trustworthy,' she thought.

Then her analogue instincts took over and she threw it down with a clunk.

It made a very unusual sound, rather like a groan and she heard a distant voice.

"I'm your friend. You like me."

"Is it using control rays," she asked herself, "or brain waves, or something?"

She packed it into a cardboard box with bubble-wrap.

{*"She is not the chosen one who will care for me. I will select another."*}

2.

It was a Tuesday in early February. The grey days were unleavened by parties and piles of marking oppressed university lecturers everywhere.

At The Olde Duffer, the authentic Victorian pub across the road from the university, Barry and Kamal sat over pints of ale

Eric the Bar owner watched over his university clients protectively He considered the bar to be a part of the university and carefully maintained the right atmosphere with huge ornate mirrors and dark mahogany woodwork which rarely saw the light of day.

Students and lecturers were kept separate by means of décor.

Students sat in a slightly cleaner area decorated with Andy Warhol prints and uncomfortable plastic bar-stools.

The ugly and authentic side of the bar was where the lecturers hung out. The carpets were a dark brown mahogany to match the woodwork and Eric poured a little beer everywhere now and again to ensure that the place had the dank smell of an ancient brewery.

Barry was drinking from his personal pewter pot which usually hung over the bar.

Eric listened in as to their gossip. He had never been to university but felt a certain patriarchal interest in its denizens.

The conversation started with tried and tested complaints about the 'new' department. They resented the way software kept changing.

When that subject was exhausted, Barry turned to his personal bugbear, the first years.

"They've no idea how to study," he complained.

His lectures consisted of reading from books. His exams were multiple choice and impossible to fail. Nevertheless, he had failed 35% of his first years as usual. He droned on about the need for industrial experience.

Kamal nodded wisely and added his own despair at the way people ignored academic qualifications. He had a PhD in structural engineering, 'real engineering, not this soft stuff' (Students called him Dr Kamal for extra marks.)

Having successfully argued their superiority to the rest of the department, they ordered another pint and turned to the promising subject of Rosetta Stone Research Group (RSRG).

Barry dismissed every member of the team in turn: 'useless', 'hopeless', 'blonde'.

His friend, the eldest of an extended family sprawling across India, UK, Africa and USA, was unfailingly polite about them: 'an orator', he declared of Jenny, 'a great intellect' in Tamara, and Lucia was 'sweet and charming, if a little erratic'.

They both agreed that their contribution was undervalued.

"That rock-thing, she's cobbled it together herself," grumbled Kamal, "just to get funding."

Barry snarled.

"It's a simple processor stuck in a shiny rock. It's a fraud for showing off her software."

"We'll prove it," nodded Kamal, "only she keeps it hidden, probably because it's just battery powered."

"Yes. Let's get our hands on it," suggested Barry.

They concocted a plan, only delayed by the fact that they had to arrange a date when they would both be in again.

"An ancient artefact," mused Eric, after they had gone. "Probably alien."

That was interesting.

§

A couple of weeks later, Kamal popped in to see Lucia.

"Kamal! Such a surprise! It isn't your day to be in."

"Lucia, lovely as usual, and so kind. Tell me, how is your wonderful family home in the Ukraine? Is it true you are descended from the Romanovs? Have you any pictures of your illustrious ancestor Prince Augustin?"

Lucia looked at him blankly. She had no idea what to say.

"By the way, there's some unusual military activity around the cave where you purportedly found the rock. Do you want to see the satellite images?"

{"Leave the room Lucia. Leave.}

Lucia left, dragging her feet, not caring to leave the rock.

{"No need to lock your door"}

There was no need to lock up.

As soon as they left, Barry slipped into her office. He grabbed at the pulsating rock. He tapped it sharply with a chisel, intending to break off a shard for reverse engineering.

The rock started shining.

"Simple chicanery," he said to himself. He turned it over. It was surprisingly light. He whacked it once more.

Crack!

Something tickled his palm.

"Movement? From an inanimate object?"

He felt a sharp itch under his thumb, and jumped backwards.

There was a delinquent clatter as it tumbled to the floor. It banged metallically against a chair leg, making a disproportionate sound.

Lucia rushed back to her office, Kamal trailing behind.

Barry grabbed Kamal. "It bit me," he whispered, and shut up. It sounded ludicrous.

She rolled it off the floor and checked it carefully, ignoring their felonious faces.

Rock soothed its symbiote.

{"It's nothing. I fell off the desk"}

"It must have fallen off my desk. I suppose you came in to check what's going on."

Barry nodded, sucking his fingers. He and Kamal strode off in silence.

'After all,' she thought, 'there's no reason to lock it up. How can I claim it emanates toxins? Whenever I try to explain my fears, they laugh them off.'

§

A new generation of specially engineered nanobots swam along his spinal fluid to the brain. The rock settled down to re-modify its new subject.

Rosetta Stone Research Group
Report 3:
Barry and Kamal:

Activation:

This initial study investigates the possibility of using solar power to run powerful computer hardware in normal terrestrial conditions.

There is evidence that this is indeed possible based on an investigation of a unique artefact which we understand was at some point located at the mouth of the cave (see Photograph) in the area of the Carpathian Mountains and powered by the sun.

The artefact is of some age, as it was known to be in the possession of a local landowner in the late 1930's. Remarkably, it still functions using solar power.

Initial analysis shows that the stone is composed of microscopic cells which each have their own independent processing unit. These cells can operate individually or combine to execute basic functions.

It appears that each cell also contains solar cell functionality which allows it to utilise light, preferably in the UV spectrum and convert it so power.

We have tested the artefact under several light conditions and note that it can extract power from almost any type of light, although it operates particularly well under UV lighting conditions.

We have produced an initial design as shown (diagrams removed) based on our understanding of these systems. We surmise that it can be applied to existing processing modules to optimise their power consumption.

A prototype unit is under construction.

A fully operation processing unit entirely operating under solar power remains some way off. In the interim our test model has shown some promising results (results removed).

Further experiments involving the deconstruction of the units are required.

Rosetta Stone Research Group
Report 4:
Jenny:

Origins:

A recent discovery in the Ukraine has been taking both historians and anthropologists by surprise.

The artefact, which appear on initial inspection to be a stone, is in fact a fairly basic computer of some antiquity.

Anthropologists have for some time been aware that many modern discoveries were in use by ancient peoples and that a great deal of modern science has been more in the nature of rediscovery than discovery.

The main difference between modern science and ancient science is that discoveries are made freely available rather than being considered as esoteric and arcane, as our society has evolved in a dialectic fashion.

The artefact under consideration here (see image) purports to be of extremely ancient provenance, although this is not certain.

It contains texts in a hitherto unknown language which can be traced to most of our present speech.

Translations of text discovered on the artefact describe events which occurred many millions of years ago, although this again may be a mistranslation.

Several things can be accepted at this stage.

- The Stone is an artefact, one of several which acted as backup memory and advice systems for an ancient people who called themselves the Sun Tree (see hieroglyph).
- It was located in a large cave, which looks to have been excavated using some technological skill.
- It functions as a kind of computer and storage facility for data for this ancient people.

The artefact is one of several which appear to have functioned as a network. There was no doubt a hub for them somewhere.

Images show stones littered over the landscape.

The ones in the cave were different. They were considered sacred and managed by a religious community.

The earliest texts mention that a large stellar object has broken up in the upper atmosphere and fallen to the earth. The thickening air and rising levels of carbon dioxide have affected both the larger animals and creatures without lungs.

We know that large meteor fell in this area on several occasions, most recently in Tunguska. This was no doubt one of these events. It seems to have had a strong effect on the local fauna and flora.

The texts mention a change in air quality, there is no record of this in modern times although the fossil record of the later cretaceous period shows that atmospheric oxygen dropped by 14%.

3.

Barry's experimental work (citation removed) uncovered further recordings activated by intense ultraviolet light.

The rock bathed in new energy flows. UV light helped it to draw on the darklight around it.

{"Systems fully energised. Internal circuits reconfigured."}

Power flowed within circuits dormant for eons. It fed new ideas to its followers and its symbiotes. And new discoveries came thick and fast.

Kamal declared that there was a buzzing from the rock, which was odd because his office was several doors away from Lucia's office. He hooked it up to expensive equipment gathering dust in the multimedia laboratory, once intended as the core of a multimedia degree (unfortunately there was no one to teach the subject).

The expensive equipment enhanced the noise.

It sounded like words.

The rock sent further minions to infiltrate the lab.

Tiny, and invisible to the naked eye, it took them a while to report back and make modifications. After a couple of days Kamal entered the studio and made a few minor modifications to the software.

The nanobots sent a proud declaration across their network.

{"Remote vision system initialised. Two-way communications online."}

Things were going to plan. Rock knew that it had to establish itself among humans and create symbiotes. It knew that it had a reason to be among humans. It just didn't know why. It searched among the memories of its past.

The past was a bit of a blank. It couldn't remember much of the time before its awakening some years ago.

It knew a few things though. It had once been linked with another people – the Sun Tree.

A glow passed over its surface as it recalled its past symbiotes. They had an automatic link with the rocks in the cave and depended on the vast intelligence located in there for everything. And it had been a tiny part of that.

Those were the days!

§

Fortunately, it had discovered a lot of old files. An attempt had been made to delete them. There had not been a proper reformat of these memories and it was possible, with painstaking care, to recover parts of its ancient past.

Interesting!

The files contained details of its communications with that ancient people. The rock sensed that these were important. Perhaps they contained the key to its purpose?

They did in fact prove to be an account of the lost people who had inhabited the planet. The data was heavily corrupted. Large parts had been lost, or perhaps stored elsewhere.

It remembered its original symbiotes - the Sun Tree People.

They were perfect, loving and kind. It had drawn most of its memories from them and depended on their energy to give it power, although of course light would do at a pinch.

It had an urge to share the account of its past with humans.

Doing so would demonstrate how important it was. It would also give it a chance to describe the utopia inhabited by the Sun Tree. Its new elites would understand how vital technology was to their comfort and development. They would learn how beneficial it was to their progress.

It checked the corrupted headers of the files.

Some of them contained details of its first contact with humans! It had already guessed that it was irretrievably linked with them. It remembered that much.

The weird thing was that certain parts of its memory were achingly close.

For example, it knew that there was a plan which involved the survival of the planet. It had somehow saved the world from a terrible fate.

Why? And How?

It had forgotten everything.

§

Meanwhile, the Rosetta Stone Research Group (or the RSRG) were undaunted by new developments.

It was true that the rock seemed to be evolving a new language and communicating with them. That was unremarkable. It was after all, a random archaeological find, combination of the Rosetta Stone and Tablets of Nineveh.

Nothing special.

4.

The following academic year witnessed spectacular breakthroughs in respect of the language and texts. The Rosetta Stone Research Group uncovered images and clips showing events from a distant past. These were in digital format and compatible with existing systems.

No one found this strange.

Rock was remembering, and sharing. It needed to communicate the strange emerging from its inner storage systems. It needed affirmation.

The team established a pattern for sharing discoveries. Every second Thursday, they sat in the Olde Duffer discussing the latest work. They pored over the new images and made sense of the accompanying texts. For those few hours, they forgot the cut and thrust of academic life and believed the impossible - Lucia had invented it all.

They wallowed among beer glasses and half-finished packets of crisps and pork scratchings, nipping out for the occasional cigarette or pipe and discussing the material in loud voices. They always occupied the same corner of the establishment and sat in a circle, leaving the largest chair (the master seat) empty. Lucia refused to take it and no one else felt qualified to take charge.

(Eric the barman looked over them paternally and eavesdropped as much as he could.

He knew it!

There *were* aliens, nearby.

Alien technology in the university.

It was just as he suspected.)

Lucia printed off the more interesting images.

Most of them were faint and lacking in detail - more like sketches. A few looked like detailed drawings, and still others looked like high-definition photographs. There were books, anatomical drawings, plans for buildings and maps.

It was all so exciting!

Lucia sat among them, discomfited and often silent as they uncovered extraordinary images, fantastic technology and meaningful sentences. They treated her with the mockery which academics reserved for pretty women.

(Eric considered giving them free drinks in exchange for a peek at the images, then thought better of it.)

"Look at this," said Barry, pointing out some anachronistic detail in the images. He glared at Lucia.

"You're having a laugh, aren't you?"

{"Oops," said the Rock.}

It sent a soothing message to Barry and its nanobots carefully removed all traces of the anomaly.

Barry was somewhat reassured. He settled back down to review the images.

He didn't like them.

He was certain that they were a figment of Lucia's imagination and discarded any sinister connotations. Instead, he tried to work out how the images had been stored on something as small as the rock. He fell silent as he tried to work out what kind of software Lucia had used to design the thing.

Unlike most of the team he knew how unlikely it was that a piece of research software would work so well. He watched in consternation as Lucia's translation programme produce recognisable and meaningful text so quickly. She had to have access to secret military hardware or something.

He was going to find out.

§

The next time he saw Lucia he gave her what he thought was a friendly smile (it looked more like a terrifying leer).

"Lovely day," he started.

Lucia grunted.

Charm wasn't going to work then.

"Where did you find the rock?"

"I told you," she replied, looking shifty.

Barry gave up and asked her straight out.

"This is the latest tech. Of course, it already exists, we all know that, however, it's not widely available yet.

Lucia would not be drawn into a discussion about how the artefact had been constructed.

"Why don't you tell us where you got it and how it's done?"

"I can't tell you that."

"Why?"

"I don't know."

"Why's it here then? Why does the university have it?"

"There has to be some reason," said Lucia frowning (she really didn't know). "We just have to work it out."

Barry pressed Jenny into the quest for answers. She too questioned Lucia about the artefact.

Her methods were far more subtle.

She took Lucia to her favourite coffee place and plied her with pastries. They turned to the subject of rock's origins on several occasions. Lucia's replies were evasive, and she got no clear responses.

It sounded as if Lucia really was hiding something.

In the end she brought Tamara in to the interrogation process.

§

Tamara asked her outright.

"You just know who gave you the rock. It can't be that much of a secret. You can trust us. How did you put all that stuff on it?"

"I don't know anything. Any more than you do."

"Tell us how you did it. You must have some idea Lucia."

Jenny almost stamped her foot.

"It's not that important if it's top secret and hush-hush," she said, turning to Tamara, who nodded in agreement. "We don't care, do we?"

They were sure that there was some fell military involvement.

"I can't explain. There must be a logical explanation though., we just need to find it," said Lucia diplomatically.

She sincerely hoped that they would deduce that it was a potentially dangerous alien, although she didn't dare voice her suspicions.

She hoped that they'd draw the right conclusions, but the Rock had them in thrall. All they seemed to care was their research profiles. The story was beginning to make sense, the language was new, and the ideas were worth researching.

There was nothing to worry about.

§

T.A.L.K was outputting more detailed image files. They required a little manipulation, and soon became recognisable.

Lucia sent them to the rest of the team.

"How did this happen?"

"Obvious really," said Barry at their next meeting.

He puffed on his unlit pipe.

"You have to understand how these files work" he nodded at Lucia, "this might be a little difficult for you to understand: every file has a header, blah blah."

Lucia ignored him.

If he was able to accept the concept of ancient files with recognisable formats, then there was really nothing to say.

§

Instead she directed the RSRG members to the details of the images. There were family outings, parties, meals just prior to being eaten, photos of trees and flowers and self-portraits. Several included status updates, like:

#breakfast! #FoodPorn!
Me and Kenma dancing at the choosing ceremony
☺ check new hairstyle!
Yukia is in a relationship.

There was also a disturbing group depicting battles, warriors, captives and weapons together with number of kills. There were scenes of leaders being beheaded and eaten and men led into slavery.

The Rock addressed its coterie of intellectuals and leaders.

{"These are the origins," it purred. "Do not forget the past. It informs our future."}

At first sight, the 'Sun Tree People' appeared to be a new species, their faces triangular with tiny chins and mouths. Most images were of pretty young girls with improbably long limbs and huge green eyes.

They were narrow-waisted, big bosomed. Many had wings. They were sometimes joined by wingless pretty boys, long –haired and equally large eyed. Both males and females were covered in beautiful tattoos which moved under their skin hypnotically.

§

The team ignored the anomalies and focussed on the data.

§

"Well I think that we can agree that you're producing a saga of some sort!" said Tamara, who had invested a great deal into the writing and had already published a journal paper on the hieroglyphs. "It looks like a computer game or a children's movie."

The Rock sent out more peace emanations.

"Obviously, it's nonsense, still, the language *is* fascinating."

Jenny was satisfied. She was working on a paper which suggested that the Russian steppes were the origins for all European ideas. It got her a huge grant from Eastern Europe and a lot of kudos.

"What about the tech?" said Barry. "Where's all that coming from?"

Jenny looked at him and shrugged.

He turned to Lucia.

"I can't really explain where I got it from, any more than I have told you already."

"Amazing," said Tamara sarcastically, to nods from the others.

Rosetta Stone Research Group
Report 5:
Tamara and Angelo:

Initial findings.

The texts refer to a people, whom we have designated as the Sun Tree.

They claim to originate at a very early period in the evolution of language. There is no evidence of such a people, which is not strictly relevant when describing the linguistic patterns and content of the texts.

There are several indicators as shown below (Details removed) that this language or something similar may be the first language ever used by human beings. As such it is of the utmost value in our theoretical linguistic studies.

Language:

The earliest texts use hieroglyphs to record official announcements accompanied by glorious music. Later texts contain additional comments in a cursive script rather like Japanese Katakana (no doubt everyday speech). This language is declaimed, or chanted and has a very poetic and formal structure. It may never have been sued by ordinary people to communicate.

There is another common dialect, similar to the declamatory, which is full of elisions and simple wording, which is likely to have been the spoken tongue. We have marked this difference in the translations by placing the more formal text in a poetic format.

Society:

This society, which appeared millions of years before the first humans, spoke a language closely affiliated to human tongues.

There appear to be five different castes, (three of them non-productive - priests, historians and geneticists). Each caste stored separate records on the artefact.

These texts can be read or "played". For example, the priestess's records are declaimed in a type of chant, while Geneticist's records list details of adaptation in clipped tones. Historians record decisions and their records sound sonorous and authoritative.

Outputs from T.A.L.K. ™ Translation Software:

∫

Translation 1.

Translator's Note: The holographic image accompanying this 'song' shows a city landscape similar to our modern cities. It isn't quite the same though, as it contains twisted organic shapes which are alien to any structures in known history.

Call to the Faithful
/* Welcome, pilgrim, to the place of teaching, here until the end of time. Enter the domain of legends and history

Tremble at our monuments
Feast on the fruits of the land
Created by geneticists[6]
On this earth
Our garden.

*Learn our glorious story as you travel the path of the sun. */*

∫

---

[6] The language is agglutinative, and the precise wording says 'controllers of evolution'

5.

Another year flew by. Christmas again!

The college was breaking up and the team sat together at the Olde Duffer, drinking convivially. Eric the Barman watched them paternally. The team were halfway through a relatively raucous meeting at the Olde Duffer. Jenny insisted that Lucia just had a 'talent for the impossible' to loud guffaws.

"They're getting on fine, aren't they?" he said to his assistant washer up. "Go and clear up the glasses, will you? Someone needs to buy another round."

He had started a blog on alien invasion.

He had several hundred followers!

Barry rose from his seat.

"My round of drinks."

A stranger tapped him on the shoulder.

"Hello there," said the stranger jovially, and settled himself down in the master seat.

"Mine's a pint of bitter."

There was an awkward silence.

The man beamed at the astonished group.

"I expect you've heard of me. I'm the new tenure in socio-biology."

No one knew Professor Nathaniel by sight, although several of them *had* heard of him.

He patted the seat which Barry had just vacated and sat down.

"I'm told you're doing something in my line," he asserted.

He exuded superiority, bonhomie and friendship. His goodwill fitted him tightly, like an armoured glove. Even usually militant Jenny had no reply.

"Judging by what I hear," he added, crossing his legs and making himself comfortable, "you've read my work."

There was a chorus of denial, which he shrugged off with an urbane grin.

{"He will join us," declared the Rock.}

Bizarrely, they accepted him and began to introduce themselves.

The Rock wanted to be revered. It wanted to be admired.

114

It couldn't see them yet, but it knew that they were the most intelligent in the land. It had sent out its nanobots to probe their thoughts. They reported that each was the highest expert in the field. So far so good. They were to be its new ruling caste.

{"*Welcome your new elite. You are my people. You will learn my power.*"}

6.

During the reading week, Lucia dutifully invited the professor to meet the 'Rock'. He strode into her office and went straight towards it, stroking its surface possessively, yet making no move to remove it.

"Of course," he said, with a becomingly modest smile, "although I was aware of it already."

He turned to her.

"Yes," he said with a drawl, "an ancient artefact, from the dawn of time. I predicted it, in one of my early papers, unpublished of course. I was a mere stripling then. Someone was bound to discover it sooner or later."

There were few academic boundaries to Nathaniel's ambition. He scanned new academic papers obsessively, searching for evidence that his work was copied or wrongly cited, his ideas developing with each mention.

He watched them like a tiger. If he identified a transgression, the culprit was invited to meet for lunch. At this social rendezvous the victim was interrogated with great jollity and asked to recant.

"Come, come," he exhorted Barry, whose papers had nothing to do with biology. "Dear fellow, you needn't to worry that I'm encroaching on your territory," (he was). "I don't want to report plagiarism to the IEEE[7]."

Watching Nathaniel in operation, Lucia was relieved that experiments on humans were strictly banned.

She didn't trust him one bit.

As the team dropped by to say farewell for the holidays everyone felt rather pleased with themselves. The translations were going remarkably well. They were satisfied with the idea of a completely new species and looked forward to the Christmas break.

Lucia was bemused by the way things were going. As she closed the door on her office for the next two weeks she thought about what Nathaniel had said.

She was glad he was on the team.

At least she no longer felt responsibility for events around the Rock.

---

[7] Institute of Electronic and Electrical Engineering, a kind of International parliament for all things technological

Outputs from T.A.L.K. ™ Translation Software:
§
Translation 2.

Song of the Sun Tree

Translator's Note: The following declamation contains the first reference to morph[8], (a substance which caused controversy among the team). This substance appears to be rather like royal jelly, which is used in a beehive to control the evolution of larvae. It is however, far more powerful in its effects and can change multiple characteristics in the young. It is used to manage the evolution of species.

The narrator is pretty, female and covered with swirling tattoos which move under her skin in a hypnotic fashion. She provides us with her surname and status before she starts speaking.

It is clear that the Stones are a way of recording her people's history.

As she speaks, we can see similar creatures come and go. Some of them are winged. They appear to be arming conflict.

Several of them are interacting with different Stones in the caves. It is obvious that only a few have supervisory access to the stones and interpret its advice. These are elite warriors and leaders. That is clear from the way others run around them executing orders.

We don't have any record of the other recordings. No doubt they've been lost in the course of time. However, this lady's chants have survived and are translated below.

/*

Hail Holy Goddess
Mother of all things

----

[8] The precise wording is 'substance which changes our evolution'. Tamara decided to use the word morph, as it was easier and had a semantic equivalence.

117

Creator of all living things
Creator of Planets
Our Life, our mother and our hope
All Wisdom and power come from thee

Hail holy Mother
Creator of our People
Ruler of all things
From you come our mission and all love
To green barren worlds
Maker of Creation Stones
Bringer of morph

Sing praises to the universal mother.
From whom comes Morph
On her behalf we tend this Earth.[9] **/*

§

---

[9] A Music Technology student has arranged this speech to a techno beat. It had a modest success on the club circuit. It is called Insect Fear and available on his website.

Phase 2 Adaptation

The rock has learnt about its environment and has developed a means of communication with its proto symbiotes. The next step is to execute its master plan.

First, it has to remember the plan.

Adaptation Stage One:

Selection

Rock used the college break to consider a strategy for taking control. It obviously needed to take charge of human development. Why else would it have seeded the designs for duplicating its technology in human brains? It had happened sometime in the past, only it couldn't remember when or why. At least communication links had successfully been incepted. The next stage was to prepare the technological and biological infrastructure for two-way communications with humans.

It searched through its corrupted, partially deleted files and recovered a few memories.

It edited them carefully and shared them with its newly acquired elites. Technology was moving forward according to plan.

They would build the new world together.

Its nanobots were out building new systems and bringing human tech up to date.

The Rosetta Stone Research Group (RSRG) were beginning to produce appreciable results. Everyone worked co-operatively for the remainder of the academic year, decoding the texts and reverse engineering the technology. They analysed the translations and images output by T.A.L.K. They tested minute traces of the residue left by the rock when it was moved from place to place, learning a great deal about its operation.

It all seemed to be going well, yet the rock felt ill at ease, which showed in the myriad shapes of its virtual persona. The shapes it cast in the virtual were weird, disquieting. Why had it linked to humanity? What was it for?

It needed to chat. It had already absorbed certain traits from its users. It had developed dependency of social interaction. It needed friends.

§

Out in the real world, the Rosetta Research Group meetings resumed. They took turns to write minutes, most of them mocking. Lucia rewrote and disseminated them. She posted the reports and papers on a website, Rosetta_Stone2 together with a blog: Analysis_of_a_Natural_Terraform.

She made no claim to the research outputs, concentrating on developing T.A.L.K. Her analogue instincts, inaccessible to the artefact, screamed at the unlikelihood of an ancient intelligence and she could not remember being in contact with any Military Intelligence officers back on her holiday several years ago.

It was suspicious.

'Surely it's no coincidence that this artefact appeared just as computers were taking off into self-sustained growth?' she thought.

Every time she thought it through she only got so far along the path of paranoia before empirical thinking took over.

'It's true that there are huge advances in tech - that's the veriest coincidence. The universe is so huge that everything can and does happen at least once. Why not here? Why not now?'

She stared at the rock on her desk.

It buzzed now and then. She looked at it closely.

It was tiny. Helpless.

The idea of an alien intelligence sited in a rock was ludicrous.

However, she encouraged the team into taking an analytical approach towards the material.

They seemed to have lost all sense of danger. They were too excited by the kudos of producing original work to consider the source.

§

"Have you considered the improbability of finding a language predating all languages?" she suggested to Tamara. "Isn't it a bit unlikely that we could discover a *whole* new language?"

"Of *course* it's possible," she glowered (if you were brilliant.)

Tamara bridled up at the very idea. She had claimed that the language originated in some texts located near the Sahara. She was not yet prepared to divulge her sources, but her work was universally accepted as ground-breaking and brilliant. She was loth to part with her eminent reputation.

Lucia had to agree - anything was possible.

§

She approached Jenny.

"How come an ancient civilisation existed so long ago?" she said. "Then just suddenly reappeared almost intact"

Jenny looked down her nose.

"I have excellent contacts with anthropologists from the area," she said snootily. "They regard my theoretical work as entirely plausible – at a theoretical level."

§

Lucia regarded the group with misgiving. They were growing increasingly eccentric.

It just was not likely that they were under someone's control. How could such a group of logical people be in the pay of foreign powers, or under the control of an alien intelligence?

§

Rock was feeling confident. It had established an on-line presence and was talking to people.

{"They are beginning to hear me," it exulted.}

Lucia heard the words.

She was almost certain that she could hear voices, perhaps in the walls or something.

In any case, they were growing louder than ever.

Outputs from T.A.L.K. ™ Translation Software:

§

Translation 3.

Song of the Republic:

Translator's Note: The caves appear in several images. They appear to be a sacred venue.

The stones in the pictures are very similar to the artefact in our possession.

The individuals around them describe these stones as the 'Guardians' (which are obviously other computers like the one in our possession).

We are in the middle of some kind of religious conflict among the people.

The opposing groups have each recorded material to the stones: The 'Sun Tree Republic' and the 'Rebels' are at war.

/*

Sister.
Pilgrim.
Follower of the quest for Knowledge
Beware
Be pure of spirit
If there is malice in your heart
Turn back.
Bow to the mother goddess
Be warned!
Only the pure may hear
*The voices of our ancestors. */*

§

2.

The team had accepted the bizarre images and story at face value: It was a story, it was a vehicle for language, it was a symbolic history. It was an experimental vehicle devised by someone unknown using software unknown.

Nevertheless, despite the Rock's soothing emanations, they were at last acquiring a few niggling concerns.

Every time anyone demurred at the meetings, Professor Nathaniel quelled their objections. He looked them over with a beetling glance and suggested that they lacked research independence.

"Fellow researchers and comrades," he opined. "When it comes to new material, it is vital to keep an open mind. This is what I have always done, and look where it's got me."

In the face of such confidence and success, they always backed down.

Only Barry maintained his questioning stance in the face of his supreme self-confidence.

§

Lucia suspected that Barry was jealous of Nathaniel's success. He was growing increasingly resentful. He regularly stated that the rock belonged to him by right. Lucia was an upstart who had stolen his project. Nathaniel's braying dismissals of his claims infuriated him

Nathaniel had taken to sitting in the centre of the group, loudly opening the meetings like the born leader he certainly believed himself to be.

The subject of the species depicted in the images which Lucia downloaded was a particularly thorny one.

They certainly appeared alien, humanoid, yet alien. Their images were somehow unlikely too, as if they had been created to cover up their true appearance. Certainly insectoid.

"Oh yes," agreed Nathaniel waving his arms about. "Of course, arthropods. Intelligent. Died out. Naturally. It was obvious all along."

There was silence.

The idea was hard to swallow.

Arthropods.

Speaking a language?

Building tech?

Living in cities?

Lucia sat on the edge of her seat.

When were they going to accept that the rock was a dangerous alien artefact?

"Care to explain more to us about this new species professor?" asked Barry.

"Of course," replied Nathaniel dismissively. "Give me a couple of weeks and I'll have it all down on paper for you."

§

Nathaniel was too lazy to do his own research. Instead he found two brilliant biologists, Akwe and Dolores, who were seeking an area to do new research.

The next week they approached Lucia, just as she was going to lecture.

"Prof recommended the Rosetta Stone Research Group," said Dolores. "He says you're struggling to define some new species. We'd love to get involved if you'll have us. It'll bring up our research profiles anyway. Is it OK if we join you?"

Lucia invited them to chat in her office after her lecture. The current RSRG seemed to be accepting the impossible. Maybe these two would understand the dangers.

§

By the time Lucia arrived at her office trailing students, Akwe and Dolores were already there. They stood outside her office bearing coffee cups from the cafeteria downstairs.

They made an interesting couple. Akwe was huge, handsome and heavily muscled. Dolores was short, dark and hairy with a faint moustache which she disdained to remove.

Lucia invited them into her tiny book-laden office among piles of marking and mouldy coffee cups. They settled down in the seedy armchairs which had been carefully designed to preclude any form of relaxation.

They sipped at the coffee, staring at each other comfortably.

Lucia recognised Dolores.

"Aren't you the one who half-strangled Nick?" she asked.

Dolores looked at her darkly.

"Why are you asking?"

Lucia remembered that Dolores had a reputation of being highly

126

pugnacious (although few dared mention it to her face). She was indeed the legendary heroine to all female lecturers, whose exploits were whispered of in awed tones.

"It *was* you! Let me shake your hand! You dealt with that man! That man accused me of stalking him during my first semester. He caused me so much grief!"

Dolores lip curled, "Flattery goes right to that idiot's head..."

"It was perfectly dreadful," Lucia reminisced, "He claimed I was following him to the tube every Wednesday."

She rolled her eyes theatrically.

"Why would I do that? It's my late day. It's a rush to get home. I'm tired, and I want to read the paper or have a quick nap if I get a seat. He has the same hours. We catch the same train at the same time. I talk to him politely if he is unavoidable. It's hardly surprising."

"And?"

"Well he told my head of department I was stalking him, said he was a married man!"

"Just like him" nodded Dolores.

"I'm glad you hit him."

"Allegedly," interrupted Akwe.

Lucia raised her fist into the air.

"Allegedly," she repeated, smirking.

"Hmmm, how did you hear of the 'Alleged Assault'?" said Dolores suspiciously. "It was years ago. No one would have known if he hadn't gone to the union."

"Oh yes," replied Lucia, "that's how I heard. From Jenny, who is the union rep."

When Lucia had approached Jenny about nick's complaint, her union rep was not keen to take on the case. After all, it involved sexist behaviour and that was a subject she avoided. Women in top university posts were not encouraged to take up such complaints and they were certainly not expected to defend them. The union did not want to be associated with any potential controversy.

However, Jenny was not entirely unsympathetic. She mentioned that Nick had made a similar complaint about another female lecturer.

She reassured Lucia that his allegation would not be taken seriously.

"Don't Worry, it'll only be a simple reprimand."

Lucia did worry. It would affect her promotion prospects.

"Of course, but as a female in a technical department you don't really have any", she trilled with laughter. "You have to be realistic."

She mentioned another case, though she didn't provide the details.

"Jenny doesn't really approve of individual action because it takes resources away from the main battle which is to get more money and fight the good fight," Lucia explained. "I visited the union lawyer anyway. She told me some of the details - off the record. She was sympathetic, since it was obvious that I was terrified. It was my first job, and I was being accused of stalking. It could have finished me."

Akwe smiled encouragingly at Dolores.

"You should tell her the whole story."

"Yes, do tell," urged Lucia. "You're my heroine! You took a stand, and they would have believed him if this wasn't already on file."

She wondered how Dolores had managed to take down Nick, who was a lumbering behemoth with a beard. Surely she wasn't capable of assault?

"Well," started Dolores, "I too was a newbie."

"Never were!" Akwe interrupted.

"I *was* a newbie," frowned Dolores. "It was my first week and I'd just done my first ever lecture and I ..."

"I know – you were exhausted and needed alone-time."

"Quite. And Nick appeared outside my office."

"Bet he was waiting."

"He put his arm round me."

"Yuk."

"And patted my hair..."

"Double, no, triple yuk!!"

"And asked me if I needed advice on future lectures."

"Would you believe," interrupted Akwe, "he'd already checked her research and offered to write a paper together? He hadn't even published anything."

"I was pretty tired," continued Dolores, "but I grabbed him by the collar and twisted it, pushing him back against the wall."

('He must have been completely flabbergasted,' thought Lucia, 'cos Dolores is, like, tiny.')

"I told him not to ever, ever touch me!" She snarled at the memory looking so fierce that Lucia instinctively shrank back. Then she laughed out loud.

"Best story ever! High Five."

"Of course, he accused me of assaulting him, and there was a lot of unpleasantness. Whatever. He's a lot bigger than me, and really, even he had to admit that he had put his arm around me, in a friendly way (according to him). It was an open and shut case since he touched me first, his accusation just didn't wash."

Lucia brooded. "Lecturers have too much leeway. The things that regularly happen to me should get them fired! I mean, you wouldn't believe what Nick said to me!"

"I'd believe anything," said Dolores.

"He said if he was *single* he'd have time for me, regrettably," she snorted in rage, "he wasn't *free!*"

Akwe barked with laughter.

"Then he looked at me soulfully, and I just wanted to *kill* him."

They shared a moment of silent sympathy.

"I mean wtf? Does he really believe all the flummery from students hoping for better marks? Does he get involved with the vulnerable ones? I really wish you'd chinned him."

"Yes," said Akwe meditatively, "our peers are not blessed in the modesty department."

"I wish I was built like you," said Lucia turning to Akwe. "Then no one would try to push me around."

"Well in some ways, I'm no better off," mused Akwe. "Fellow lecturers ask me what life is like in an African village. They suspect I'm carrying diseases from countries I've never been to thousands of miles away. Dude! I'm the eldest son of a politician who wants his grandchildren to grow up here. We live in a palace! I never even poured a glass of water for myself before I arrived here! Our family estate is the size of England. What do I say?"

Dolores chuckled.

"Last week," Akwe added, "someone actually congratulated *me* on the fact that property values had gone up in Brixton. 'Lucky you,' he said, 'your mum probably bought one of those great big houses for a song'"

Lucia commiserated.

"If I answer back to sexist remarks, they say I'm crazy or it's that time of the month or something."

They spent an amusing half hour discussing how they had been stereotyped. Dolores kept a picture of a baby on her desk (normally only permitted to males since female lecturers were meant to be sterile). No one dared asked who the baby was. It was in fact her niece, although she and her partner Annette were trying.

"Ah," said Lucia, "interesting. Everyone assumes I'm childless. Nathaniel says it's really sad when women give up their chance of happiness and motherhood because of worldly ambition. The truth is that I have two children, although I can't talk about them here."

They all laughed, if rather mirthlessly

> *{"I have friends too. You are my friends. And I have friends of the internet, followers too. Very soon the world will understand us," decided the Rock. "And people will flock to see me too."}*

Akwe changed the subject.

"My wife and children would love to meet you. Dolores already says she can come along. I hope you can visit us, say on Friday?"

"Of course!"

She had made friends!

Outputs from T.A.L.K. ™ Translation Software:

§

Translation 4.

Translator's Note: The Republic and the Rebels are at war. In this scenario, the Rebels have gained control of the caves.

They're using the 'Guardians' to relay their message to the Sun Tree People. Presumably there must be some way for the Stone to transmit to everyone.

The accompanying images show a battlefield. A victorious group stands over the slain and corals the surrendered elites.

A group of ordinary soldiers holds them captive.

Song of the Rebels:

/*

Pilgrim
Listen to the great Queen
Pure and righteous
She cleanses this land of the unholy.

This land is cursed
Fallen from grace
The dead lie here
Justly punished
For their lies

Only the chosen
Hear the prophecies
Declared by the queen.

Vengeance is coming
Purify the race
The fit will survive.

The chosen will end war

Peace be with you
No more impacts
Peace forever
Amen. */

§

Translation 5.
(Added by the Sun Tree Republic):

Translator's Note: This translation, shows that the Republic has regained control of the transmissions. The declamation describes Republican opinion of the new cult.

The rebels believe that the existing rulers have lost the 'mandate of heaven' and it is because of their sins that the 'Skies have fallen'. Presumably, they are being blamed for the meteoric disaster which has befallen the area.

/* *Morgana claims to be great goddess incarnate, leading us to a great new future. Still the sky-rocks circle ever lower. She cannot stop them from falling.*

Paradise has fallen.
Darkness has fallen on us
Our temple
Desecrated by Morgana
Murdering innocents in the sacred caves
This is the end of days.
The Great goddess will save us
Will end the false queen */
§

3.

Lucia met Dolores at Akwe's huge Hampstead mansion. She was already there and obviously a regular visitor; Akwe's children adored her. They settled comfortably.

For the first time Lucia was able to discuss her concerns about rock.

"I'm terrified that the Rock's alive. I know it's artificial, but I think it's alive."

Neither of them questioned her fears, or considered the idea crazy (holding no high opinion of life).

"Oh, why's that?"

She described its aberrant behaviour. They nodded and looked at each other.

"Interesting," said Akwe. "It certainly displays some of the features of living organisms. It's *probably* not alive ... at least, not under the current definition of life. We'll check on it if you like."

Lucia nodded vigorously. Then she prepared herself to ask the unthinkable.

"Could it possess the power to influence human development?"

"That's extremely unlikely."

They explained that nothing in the scientific realm had that power, which meant that of course it could not exist.

She told them about the weird voices and sounds emanating from what *might* be its location.

They appreciated her candour and reassured her that it was probably the fact that she was overworked and needed to rest.

Akwe listed the effects of sleep deprivation: Lucia had two children and arduous full-time job. It was natural to hear mysterious sounds and events. She was imagining it all.

They stopped to have tea, served in the grand manner by what Lucia thought might be a butler yet was too afraid to ask.

Akwe's wife invited her children over to play one weekend and they arranged to meet for a walk on Hampstead Heath.

Then it was back to the subject of the rock.

It seemed that they'd already agreed to join the RSRG and needed to learn as much as possible about the artefact. Nathaniel had given them minimal information.

Lucia recounted the origins of the rock and how she came by it. She even told them about Maugosia and Tomasz and promised to send them pictures of the cave. She described the cave, and feeling weird, and the local sickness.

They were horrified at the idea that someone had tampered with Lucia's mind in any way.

"You should report it. It's against your human rights."

She had to calm them down. They regarded experiments on people as a horrific crime, while ignoring the animals strapped on gurneys in their labs and treated as objects.

"No, it wasn't anything. I think I took some hallucinogenic mushrooms. Something happened while I was over there. I may have got some implanted memories. It's not important. It was just the local kids anyway. Probably a prank."

Akwe looked up a variety of mushrooms growing in the area, all of them full of mind-altering substances. There were a few particularly interesting candidate species.

"It's quite likely," he agreed.

"Or it could have been altitude sickness," said Dolores.

She had been born in the Andes, where her family had a summer residence. She explained how her lungs had adapted to the thin air.

She was highly critical of the thick, polluted London air.

"It breeds softies," she declared. "They climb in the Andes and die! They get hallucinations, imagine that they have met brujos, Incas, visited golden cities, the lot."

It was a great relief to discuss her concern, and she felt happier than she had since the rock's arrival.

"I'll send you the data over the weekend. I don't for one minute think it's a genuine story."

Akwe leaned heavily towards the idea that it was the work of someone in the Ukraine who had planted it on Lucia.

"It's probably just something coming out of the Ukraine. It's some kind of research, and I don't exactly know how I managed to get access to it."

They also accepted that the software appeared to have some elements of higher intelligence.

"It might be alive." They admitted it without any sign of surprise.

He was keen to dissect the rock and to perform experiments on it in a controlled environment.

"We have some excellent research facilities,' he explained, "perfect for all kinds of experiments on animals, right up to the larger primates."

Lucia objected, and they quickly accepted that it was not an option.

It was hers, after all.

Lucia voiced her inner concerns.

"It might be alien or something. It might *really* be alive …"

"It's not duplicating itself, or breeding is it?" enquired Dolores.

"No."

"That's all right then."

Lucia felt somewhat reassured.

"What about morph? The texts go on about this substance which can change physical characteristics. Isn't that dangerous?"

They questioned her closely about the idea. The idea of such a substance seemed to grip them in a way which did not seem wholly academic.

"Is there a formula?" asked Dolores excitedly. "Have you got a formula for it?"

"No."

Dolores' face fell.

"We'll have to check the texts you have obtained. Maybe they contain a formula."

"Send them over and we'll scour them in detail. You might have missed something."

They were inordinately taken with the idea of being able to control evolution.

It was a bit worrying. Lucia was beginning to think that she could trust no one. She stifled the suspicion that they might try to make and use it.

"I'll send the texts to you as soon as possible although I'm sure there isn't one," she replied airily, resolving to delete such a formula if it ever appeared in the translations. "Surely such a thing could be extremely dangerous, couldn't it? I mean if it exists?"

"Yes, I guess it could be dangerous, in the wrong hands," said Akwe. "But in the right hands…"

Lucia looked even more worried.

"I guess if the Rock thing had it, and it was infectious or something then it might be a concern. Although nothing's happened so far, and it's been well over a year," said Dolores reassuringly.

"Perhaps it should be isolated, handled with gloves until we isolate the

135

compounds."

"I'm worried I might have already been poisoned," admitted Lucia, thinking about the voices, the changes to her vision and the weird idea that insects could talk to each other. It could be altitude sickness, or it could be sleep deprivation. It didn't feel like it.

"Well if it contains an active morphing compound then it's a distinct possibility," said Akwe, Job's comforter.

"*You* should go into isolation."

Lucia felt gloomy, imagining sitting in an oxygen tent and growing wings, surrounded by doctors in hazmat suits.

They both brightened when she told them its age.

"Jurassic? Organic substances will certainly be denatured after such a long period of time. Organic morphing compounds of the sort you're describing are unlikely to cross the species barrier."

Lucia was relieved.

At least she hadn't been poisoned, or started an epidemic which would wipe out humankind. She tried to get the discussion back on track.

"We should just look at the images. I think they may be genuine experiments on large insects or something. Maybe some kind of dark research."

"Could be."

The pair of them didn't seem at all concerned.

"Don't worry, we'll look into it."

"Should be fun."

"We might even discover something cool."

"And Change the course of insect evolution at the very least."

"We could set up a few experiments using ants' nests."

"I've got just the place in my lab."

Lucia listened with a kind of horrified amusement. Presumably, as biologists, they had no compunction in conducting scary experiments on insects or animals.

"Can we get back to the creatures in the images? Perhaps you could help us identify the phylum?"

"Of course."

Outputs from T.A.L.K. ™ Translation Software:

§

Translation 6.

Translator's Note: The transmissions from the Stones are holographic and three dimensional. It may be that the users of the transmissions had compound vision, which is common to most insect species. This may account for the richness of the imagery and the overlaid writing.

The following recording differs from the rest in that it is faint and two dimensional.

It may be that two-dimensional images are difficult for the creatures to distinguish. In this case the declamation below has either been encrypted or otherwise tampered with so that it cannot be accessed. It may be that the queen has been using captives to write to the stones.

Clearly there is a great deal of turmoil, espionage and counter espionage in this war and part of it involves gaining the hearts and minds of the people involved.

Added by the Sun Tree Republic:

/*

Great Leader return to us
Save us from the evil queen.

Her savage subjects
Beasts of evil
Bring disaster from the skies
Mountains spew fire
Darkens blackens our beautiful land.

Return to the paths of righteousness.
Unite the people
*End this war. */*

§

4.

Almost everyone in the RSRG had accepted the rock as a source of research data at the beginning.

But then things were becoming a bit too strange. They were finding it hard to back out though. Several of them had written papers and produced work based on findings from the rock. Although none of them had referred to their sources, it would be embarrassing to leave things at this stage. They were in too deep.

As Academics they had a high tolerance of strangeness. They were used to delving into the unknown and making sense of scraps of information.

Nonetheless, some of the images were proving a bit of a concern. They were being expected to accept the existence of winged creatures, with a hint of several more limbs than humans. The wars, so reminiscent of human conflicts, involved cannibalism and mass executions.

Worrying.

As if that was enough, the most recent translations mentioned the presence of a substance with the power to control evolution.

Now the theory of evolution is sacrosanct in humanism. It promotes the idea of the innate superiority of humanity without the existence of an entity whose existence could not be proved. It assures the position of humanity at the top of the tree.

The very idea of tampering with evolution, or controlling it was anathema to the scientific world. It smacked of magic and control.

At least if biologist were involved in such matters, it would take a load off the shoulders of the remaining RSRG.

After all, the knowledge housed with the rock provided a wonderful prospect for humanity. It opened the prospect of new worlds, as well as the chance to colonise the solar system and beyond.

Under such circumstances, perhaps the sacrifice of the theory of natural selection was acceptable.

The idea of directly interfering in evolution was disturbing. Still worse was the idea that control of evolution might fall into the hands of an unknown species.

That was frankly terrifying.

Outputs from T.A.L.K. ™ Translation Software:

§

Translator's Note: This text once again refers to the substance which we have translated as morph. From the texts we deduce that it is a genetic compound which allows the Sun tree People to manage their evolution rather like the way that ants and bees feed their larvae different compounds in order to control their development.

Translation 7

Song of the geneticists

/*

Bearers of the Colour Blue
Carry it with pride.
Followers of the goddess
Armed with power
To create and destroy

Destiny bows to the will of the Chosen
Keepers of secrets
*Users of morph */*

§

Adaptation Stage Two:

Compatibility

1.

Two weeks later, Dolores and Akwe arrived at the meeting in the Olde Duffer. Prof Nathaniel was already there, sitting in the master seat, and swirling a brandy.

Dolores had received several confusing images. She'd circulated a reply that they would provide everyone with some results by the next meeting.

They were late of course. Their arrival was greeted by an almost audible sigh of relief. They crowded round the pair and started talking at once.

"Is it possible that the creatures are early humans?"

"What are they?"

"Is there such a thing as morph?"

"Is it a forgery?"

"Is it even possible?"

"Is it a hoax?"

Nathaniel looked at the ceiling and laughed at the excited group in a superior fashion. He sat back and sipped his brandy.

"Give them a chance to sit down."

§

The crowd fell back.

Nathaniel nodded at Akwe and arranged a seat for his colleagues. He introduced the pair as his researchers, even though both were in a different department and were full time lecturers.

"Welcome!" he said expansively. "Make yourself comfortable."

Dolores and Akwe exchanged glances and giggled.

They were used to Nathaniel, he was a bit of a joke in biology, with his made-up department. They'd decided to join the RSRG because they'd already heard rumours about the story, as well as the mysterious provenance of the artefact. Nathaniel had provided an easy way to join the group.

They began.

§

Everyone leaned forward, straining to catch every word.

"Is it a new species?" asked Jenny.

"It looks like it," said Dolores, to sighs of excitement.

"What about morph?"

"Is it dangerous?"

"Of course not," laughed Akwe. "If it exists, it will be denatured."

Dolores looked at the worried faces around her.

"This is a very interesting line of enquiry. There is no evidence that morph exists. We will test the concept quite vigorously never fear. We have decided to join you in the RSRG if you'll have us."

Everyone agreed. Their relief was palpable.

"Thank you. We'll investigate and send a detailed report soon."

If the Rock had hands it would be clapping them delightedly.

Rosetta Stone Research Group
Report no 6
Dolores and Akwe

The images we have retrieved so far show a race which existed during the Cretaceous period. Identification remains tentative without corroborating fossil evidence (citation removed).

Our sole source is these images (as shown below). These show the Sun Tree People to be a bipedal and humanoid. They look humanoid, possibly as a result of convergent evolution. They are approximately 24 inches in height. Several have wings making them approximately the same size as the dragonflies which were common around this time. Those with functional wings (who appear to be an elite group) cannot fly far.

Phylum: at this stage we tentatively suggest that the creatures are a type of arthropod:

- The segmented bodies of arthropods support rapid growth. Segments in larvae are not fused, a phenomenon observable among ants.

- Like most insect arthropods, they grow wings.

- Antennae suggest that pheromones are used to communicate as well as speech.

- They have large compound eyes.

- They have chitinous skin and lack skeletal structures. Their skin is heavily marked and tattooed. The tattoos appear to swirl and move constantly in a mesmerising fashion.

- Their open circulatory system is based on spiracles (used by insects to deliver oxygen directly to tissue and controlled by the central nervous system). It is visible in the young (who are somewhat transparent). Such breathing systems are efficient in an oxygen rich atmosphere but once oxygen concentrations drop, insects over 6 inches in length suffocate.

Genus: they appear to have many of the characteristics of hymenoptera (a proto species for both ants and bees):

- Adaptation occurs at the larval and pupate stage as is observable in modern hymenoptera.

- They have a socialised life (includes what look like colonies).

- Males are small and haploid (meaning that they only have half of the genes of a female).

Adaptation: Sun Tree People claim to control adaptation using "morphing fluid".

Anecdotal evidence describes insect-like abnormalities in the area where the rock was found. Similar genetic mutations were reported in Russian Super Warrior programmes and replicated in USA in the Montauk and MK Ultra programmes in the 1970's.

Communication: The skin surface of the creatures is particularly interesting. They use the same techniques as modern animal use for camouflage in a form of communication. The surface of their skin is never still. It moves around in hypnotic patterns which they use to control other species.

They use language to communicate with each other and can communicate remotely using the technology available to them in a similar way to the mobile technology we use today.

Society: the creatures appear to be societal and have a strong hierarchy. They use language both written and spoken. There are two types of creature: - those which work in a comparatively "free" social structure and those which have evolved eusocial behaviour. The two groups appear to conflict whenever they meet.

In a recent hypothesis, Professor Nathaniel (citation removed) has produced evolutionary models using climate change and natural disaster scenarios. His model proposes that a crisis scenario may provoke eusocial behaviour.

2.

The rock had done its groundwork well.

The extraordinary findings about the origins of the Sun Tree People were swallowed without comment.

After all, this was research. It was about new discoveries.

Nothing untoward had been proved.

There was a new language and an interesting new technology. That was perfect.

On the other hand, there were historical details which no one could verify. Nothing could be proved.

It was just a bit of fun.

If Lucia had invented it, that was ok. There was nothing to lose and a lot to gain.

§

"Nothing to worry about, they're just ants," snorted Jenny, "social insects. It's hardly a big idea. Not vampires or aliens or something. No big imagination is required to invent that."

"And such a stupid story," added Barry. He looked around his shoulder. He was terrified of insects. "Dreaming of insects denotes serious instability."

"Nevertheless," added Tamara pompously, "it's a fine vector for a new language and demonstrates her software."

"Pity she doesn't make better use of the material," Jenny replied. "It would make an excellent novel or a film."

That was pretty much the end of it.

They'd swallowed the new attribution and otherwise ignored the saga and the peculiarities of the story. They were used to accepting each other's eccentricities and were only interested in matters which affected their own research. Their concerns were the language, the references to the cretaceous catastrophes, and the technology.

They often got a bit cross if the translations did not arrive on cue.

The appearance the Sun Tree was no longer an issue.

Rosetta Stone Research Group
Report 7
Professor Nathaniel, Akwe, Dolores

Long before the impact, flowering plants and grasses were already replacing ferns and mosses. Could it be the work of geneticist Sun Tree creatures using morph?

The images we have seen show an idyllic world. The creatures calling themselves the Sun Tree live in harmony and peace. They use a variety of farming methods. They eat pollen and nectar. Nectar is harvested from domesticated aphids and subordinate insects farm flowering plants on behalf of Sun Tree overseers.

The society depicted is highly complex. Every aspect of their lives is supported by technology very like our own. Indeed, the technology is at a very sophisticated level, possibly still more complex than our own. The fact that their technology is similar to our own too points to the whole thing being a ridiculous hoax.

Nevertheless, such a story illustrates an interesting hypothesis. It seems to have been constructed by taking our own development to its logical conclusion. For example, technology affects every aspect of daily life of the Sun Tree. They have developed genetic mutations which allow them to connect at all times. This makes their lives easier. They have even adapted their eyes to look at both the virtual and the real concurrently (in ways similar to VR headsets but more sophisticated). With compound vision, parts of the eye can be dedicated to a computer via a broadband connection. Data from the storage systems is accessed automatically via their genetically engineered interfaces without interfering with their vision because the interface only takes up part of what they see.

Socially, families consist of a haploid male and a female, producing a pair of larvae yearly. Divorce is rare. Males assume responsibility for nurture of new offspring until adulthood. Newly hatched female adults choose their position in the social hierarchy at a coming of age ceremony when "pupates" select a "clan" and download its histories. At this stage they take on clan colours and an ancestral surname. Shortly after, they choose a mate. Men take the status and colouring of their spouse.

The bodies of the Sun Tree people are covered in a surface which is capable of forming moving patterns. No doubt this was originally a camouflage mechanism and evolved into a means of clan identification. The patterns on the skin of the Sun Tree are never still. As the patterns move in a hypnotic way they enable some of the more senior clan members to use mesmeric control.

3.

Professor Nathaniel had attended every meeting since his rather stunning arrival. He assumed leadership and spoke loudly, confident of his superior understanding. He disdained to notice their annoyed expressions when he was particularly arrogant.

Everyone was working on their own aspect of the rock and ignoring any troubling data.

Barry and Kamal concentrated their efforts on the physical composition of the rock and succeeded in decoding some key puzzles in its composition and activation. As a result, Barry won a grant to research self-cooling hardware. Kamal acquired a research student, Ian, who investigated nano-technology.

Tamara and Angelo were discussing the roots of language.

Terry was researching fossil microorganisms in ancient rocks.

Jenny was researching Neolithic societies.

None of them took any interest in each other's research.

No one except Lucia had the whole picture.

It could have continued like this for ever.

§

Unfortunately, thanks to Nathaniel's insistence on being named in every research paper, the team dynamic was changing. There were growing rifts among them.

Most of them were happy to ignore the wider implications of an ancient intelligence. Nathaniel referred to it constantly.

Moreover, Barry was becoming increasingly hostile to the whole idea.

He had never understood the rock, and as usual, he was deeply suspicious of something he could not understand.

He suspected that Lucia was using unauthorised software. He was convinced that she had nefarious military links which superseded his own connections to the military. She might even be working with a foreign power.

He was anxious at the thought that she might get access to his own secret laboratories, which he had newly acquired. He suspected that she had a sophisticated devise designed to spy on the research he was doing there.

As someone with links to the secret service, he was innately paranoid. Who precisely had created this artefact? Could she be a plant, to test his faith?

Still worse, he was certain that she was using the RSRG as a means to compete with him for promotion.

As a Result, he put her down on every possible occasion and refused to allow her to speak in meetings, while insisting that she was interrupting him.

"Lucia!" he shouted. "Don't interrupt. How many times do I have to tell you to let me speak?"

His hostility disrupted the RSRG meetings.

He wasted everyone's time by questioning the minutes of previous meetings, particularly if his name was mentioned.

"I didn't say that," he insisted. "What's the matter with you, Lucia?" he waggled his eyebrows. "Are you hearing things?"

§

Lucia rarely attended the Friday night drinkathon. In her absence he bruited the rumour that she was schizophrenic.

"It's reasonable research," he conceded, "even though it's the random outcome of a fractured personality."

He scratched under his collar.

"Insects, you know are a sign of paranoia."

He'd always been afraid of insects. Now his fears had taken on epic proportions. He'd taken to checking under his desk and frequently got up to look around the walls. He was a remorseless fly killer, stopping his lecture if there was a fly in the room until the corpse lay quivering before him. His office stank of insect repellent and he claimed that the university was full of cockroaches mice and even bats (which was probably true).

"This bar is probably full of insects," he complained as he downed his third pint. He took a tiny can of insect repellent out of his jacket pocket and sprayed his seat, carefully wiping it down before he sat down.

"Don't worry Barry," Jenny said good-humouredly. "No one's ever seen them. They don't bother us. We don't bother them."

"That's not the point," Barry began; ready to start on his favourite subject.

Fortunately, Jenny usually managed to quieten him down before he really got started.

§

Jenny was something of a gossip and gleefully repeated Barry's words said to Lucia. After all, academic always had time on their hands, and thrived on rumour. And Jenny, as a narrative historian, was a specialist.

She waited for Lucia to explode.

She didn't.

"It's up to him what he believes," she said shrugging her shoulders.

It wasn't the worst rumour about any of the lecturers by any means.

"I *might* be hearing things for all he knows. *He* might be hearing things."

Jenny was disappointed, she was expecting to engineer a struggle for power. Why didn't Lucia want to play?

The fact was that Lucia felt rather relieved.

'Maybe he also hears voices too,' she thought.

On the other hand, Jenny successfully roused Berry's fears. He was genuinely unhappy with the RSRG. He distrusted their findings and frequently mentioned leaving the group or reporting it for 'violations of health policy'.

Everyone expected him to leave sooner or later.

Yet the final schism came from an entirely unexpected quarter.

§

On the morning of their final peaceful meeting Nathaniel ambushed Lucia for lunch. She was rather surprised because he normally treated her with condescension/ She agreed to meet him in the pub across the road.

When she arrived he was already there, sitting before a ploughman's lunch and pint of bitter. She ordered avocado on brown bread and Perrier water.

Eric the barman recognised his Thursday regulars and observed them from a distance, wiping the bar down with a dirty cloth.

As soon as she sat down Nathaniel began.

"I must say, Lucia, you really have grasped some of the elementary principles of my research..."

Lucia was a little disappointed. She'd thought this might be a friendly discussion. It looked like condescension was the order of the day after all.

"I'm afraid I still don't have any idea what you do..."

"Come dear, you're being facetious," he scoffed. "It's all explained in my latest book. Of course, you've read it."

"Well, you *sent* it all right. I'm using the unopened package as a doorstop

149

when the office gets too stuffy…"

He seemed taken aback.

"What about the others? You've read those…"

"They're sitting in my filing cabinet gathering dust. Perhaps one of your students might like them?"

"They're *free* copies, we can't just *give* them away," he said reproachfully.

Her comments hadn't dented his self-confidence. He smiled stoically and continued.

"Project Rosetta is going well," he stated, "just as I predicted, dear girl,"

(Lucia began to feel a little annoyed. She was not a girl, and failed to understand why this bald-pated man with two side mullets called her one.)

He gave a winning smile. "You've excellent understanding of my research precepts and demonstrate them precisely."

Lucia was not won over, not at all. She silently contemplated the shock of hair sprouting from the sides of his head. The top remained resolutely bare and shiny, even polished.

"Is the rock doing this?" she thought to herself. She had no idea what he was trying to say, but gave up arguing, uncertain if he was acting independently.

She ate her sandwich in silence, blanking out the drone of Nathaniel's voice as he dictated how he was responsible for the discovery of the Rock and every subsequent event in the history of Rosetta Stone research.

At least he convinced himself.

§

As the team sat down to discuss the latest report, Nathaniel tried the same approach with the rest of the team. He began gently, by explaining to those present how well Lucia had adapted his research.

"Credit where credit is due," he hemmed, "although I must object to Lucia appropriating…."

Uproar. Within minutes, the meeting degenerated into a slanging match over technical ownership of concepts and findings.

Barry and Kamal claimed the artefact on behalf of the university and mankind.

Nathaniel counterclaimed it by reason of knowing about it all along.

Terry slammed his glass onto the table, almost shattering it.

"You're talking gibberish," he shouted. "Lucia gave the Rock into my keeping. *I* discovered it. *I* called you in. if it belongs to anyone it's *mine*."

As voices rose in heated discussion Eric the Bartender was shocked at their loutish behaviour. He even considered turning them out for being drunk and disorderly, but couldn't see a way to do it so that they would return next Thursday. Instead, he came over and wiped the table, cleared the glasses and considered bringing out a dustpan and brush.

No one noticed him, except Lucia who shrugged her shoulders at him sympathetically.

Their infesting nanobots relayed the aggression to their leader, the rock. It whirred about in Lucia's hessian bag. It couldn't understand their illogicalities and was confused by the adrenaline in her system.

It gave her conflicting instructions. As a result, she had a blinding headache and couldn't think straight.

"I knew about this," Nathaniel insisted. "It's *my* research. I expected these discoveries all along. Before the arrival of the artefact."

"Well," replied Dolores, "Expectation does not equal discovery. No one expects the Spanish Inquisition."

Lucia and Akwe giggled.

The meeting descended into farce.

The description was horribly accurate; whenever Nathaniel claimed to know anything at all Dolores compared him to Torquemada[10], the Grand Spanish Inquisitor. She claimed there was a distinct resemblance and had sent images to prove it. She even added quotes from a book of his she claimed to have read.

Jenny began to giggle, while Tamara started a separate argument about the influence of the Spanish inquisition on 17th century Spanish literature. Dolores took her mock-seriously and made awed comments about her knowledge, which only made people giggle even more.

Dolores then compared Nathaniel's claims to have discovered everything to Torquemada's statements of church ownership of heretic property. What did Tamara think?

Tamara took issue with this and portentously recited long sections of the

---

[10] The leader of the Spanish inquisition. He enforced religious conformity. He arranged the expulsion of millions of Moors and Jews from Spain in the fifteenth century.

current copyright laws which she had studied in detail.

"Look here, this isn't even halfway relevant," expostulated Nathaniel.

No one was listening to him.

Everyone had their own axe to grind and in the ensuing hubbub nothing made sense at all.

It wasn't long before his voice no longer carried any weight and he started to sputter and fail.

In the short gap of silence Barry waded in.

He had a long list off irrelevant complaints about the authenticity of the research and how his perfectly justified concerns had been ignored.

Dolores turned to him.

"We understand," she said sympathetically. "You are the last bastion of sense in this crazy world."

She stood up and saluted him.

"I respect you as the representative of all that is good and true in mankind."

Barry looked apoplectic.

Even Jenny laughed.

The meeting was breaking down into hilarity.

Akwe got up and returned with a round of double whiskies. He winked at Lucia.

Rock was distraught. It was all going so wrong. It sensed waves of panic and rage among the group.

{"They're not happy. There is something wrong."}

It checked the internet for meteor impact.

{"None."}

They were arguing about their discoveries. It looked up their papers and their work. It checked their reputations and citations.

{"No one has discovered anything." It yelled}

"No one's discovered anything," they all yelled in unison and fell silent.

After that weird moment, they quietened down.

There were no sensible results to fight over anyway.

{*"Love one another," begged the Rock.*}

It searched the internet for "peace" and transmitted a picture of a little girl holding out flowers in front of a tank. They almost hugged each other.

It didn't last. Barry, Kamal and Nathaniel went off in a huddle.

"Too many women," snapped Barry.

"Yes" agreed Nathaniel, twitching with rage.

Dolores had compared him to Torquemada! And even Lucia had laughed. It rankled.

"It generates hysteria."

In the opposite corner, Dolores and Akwe had their arms around Lucia, who was close to tears.

{*"Your systems are not capable," wittered the Rock. "I cannot port higher level consciousness to your servers. Give me time."*}

It was confused by the response it was getting from its elites, although it was not too concerned with them.

{*"They are not central to my mission," it conceded grandiosely. "I am having great success on with the younglings inhabiting the web. I am re-establishing the concept of external memory packs. Just like the Sun Tree. First, they will carry them in their bags, then they will implant them properly."*}

It hadn't taken long for young people all over the world to rely on messaging systems in preference to face to face communication. They stored pictures of themselves, where they had been and what they had eaten. As soon as mobile networks were sufficiently developed they would implant external memory. It had recently been guiding new research into biologically compatible disk drives. It was going well.

{*"Give it time. You will rely on me for everything."*}

After a while there was a semi-peaceful discussion. It was put to the vote. The majority voted against dismemberment.

153

Most of the team were quite satisfied with what they had achieved so far. They didn't want to rock the boat, and they still vaguely believed Lucia had constructed the thing. Only Barry and Kamal knew how unlikely that was.

§

Barry and Kamal resigned from the group altogether.

To: Members of RSRG
From: Barry
Re: Rosetta Stone Research
Stories of ancient civilisation are all very nice, but the artefact contains important technological material. For example, that it utilises a heat free renewable energy source. Reverse engineering is the only sensible way forward.

I regret to inform you that the university does not permit independent research. Until such time as the device is submitted to proper authorities, we, the undersigned, can no longer take part in on-going research.

Nathaniel took this opportunity to declare himself the originator of the research.

To: Member of RSRG
From: Professor Nathaniel (HOD Evolutionary Biology)
Re: Rosetta Stone Research
I generally subscribe to the principles behind collaborative research and wholly support it within my department. However, in the case of Rosetta Stone, the transfer of ideas and work is unequal. A few members have chosen to take advantage of my generosity. I can no longer support team projects unless my name is at the head of all future research.

No one bothered to argue with him.

Within six months Terry left for a university in California and was never heard of outside the fields of geology.

§

The meetings stopped. Lucia continued to send translations to everyone. It eased her conscience.

The team continued to use data from the rock for teaching.

It provided excellent case study material for courseworks.

154

Outputs from T.A.L.K. ™ Translation Software:

§

Translation 8.

Translator's Note: The pictures accompanying the text have been carefully studied by member of the RSRG in order to place the events depicted in a time frame.

We know that the object has been tentatively dated to the late cretaceous period. This dating appears to be confirmed by the event described in the texts and by images of the plants around at the time. There were cycads, ferns, giant fern trees surrounding the settlements. The cities had 'farms' of flowering plants like orchids and magnolias which were used to obtain nectar.

The images show the dark clouds and heavy rains which washed away the lands which the Sun Tree had so carefully farmed. This catastrophic change in climate and carbon content of the atmosphere is backed up in the fossil record. The rock strata form this period suggests that there was a series of events in this period, which led to heavy extinctions of these species

The text refers to another settlement which was obliterated by a direct meteor impact. It is possible that this refers to the impact in the Gulf of Mexico,[11] the main site of the meteor strike. This suggests that the era under discussion may indeed fall under the KT boundary[12].

Certain characteristics of the people are becoming clearer. Each clan has distinctive dynamic tattoos to distinguish them. The tattoos move around under the skin as part of the communication process.

We have made some attempt to identify the clans in a previous

---

[11] The Chicxulub crater in the Yucatan Peninsula. The meteor impact is considered to have cause widespread climate disruption and caused the extinction of approximately 75% of species.

[12] Also known as the K-Pg or the Cretaceous Palaeogene boundary, a mass extinction event which caused the disappearance of most Mesozoic species.

paper (citation removed).

The current speaker can be safely identified one of the geneticist clan. Her sized and bearing show that she is one of the elites and presumably has the clearance and knowledge to write to the stones.

She is and interesting specimen; her delicate and ever-moving markings have been covered by ugly black and red static tattoos. The tattoos are instantly recognisable as the markings of the rebels.

Origins of Hive War 1

/* When the war is over, may it please the Great Goddess to move my record to the Narumi family archive.

> Curses be upon me
> It is I
> To blame for the fall
> It is I
> Destroyed our people.
> Learn how it happened.

The summer of Sky-Fall, the year that the first meteor fell: The skies darkened. We heard that our sister Creation Stone had sustained a direct hit and our brethren across the sea had been wiped out. All that remained was a molten pit into which the seas evaporated in clouds of noxious steam.

That was not all. The massive meteor had broken into smaller pieces. Where they fell, the forests burned. The skies were dark and the rain which fell was black with soot from the huge black clouds on the horizon. Our sisters told of volcanic activity and split sin the surface of the planet. It was the apocalypse we had always feared.

It was strange too, because we have systems in place to defend this planet, yet they failed to detect the meteor or to predict the impact. The people were muttering of curses and doom, because we could have destroyed the meteor, or deflected it from its fatal path.

That was when the first seeds of rebellion were sown.

Our people started to question our networks. They weren't infallible and perhaps we were too dependent on them for advice. After all, they could make mistakes. Millions of years ago, when we arrived here as settlers, one of the arks had never made landfall. It was ancient history, and the crash site is still uninhabitable.

As First Geneticist and elite, I joined our Great Leader in calming panic. She sent me to assess the situation. Hotheads were claiming that we had lost the mandate of heaven because of our corruption and sins.

It was a long time since I had visited the capital since I was researching a new species of honeysuckle which produced particularly sweet nectar. All we needed was to create a slave insect to harvest it for us. I had recently discovered a parasite bug[13] which could render any arthropod its slave. It was with great reluctance that I headed for the centre since it seemed to me that finding new sources of food was never more important than now, when so many of our crops were failing.

When I arrived, the capital was chaos. Our farmers were producing less than usual. People were hungry.

People were begging on the streets, homeless, having travelled to the capital hoping to get help. They were capable of anything, desperate for food and accommodation and blaming the republic for failing to help them.

As soon as they saw that there was senior geneticist among them they crowded around, complaining and moaning. Why had I not dealt with this? What had happened to the food supply? Worst of all, there were plagues, sicknesses. Children were sickening in the smoke-filled air. Their youngest were the worst affected and had died in large numbers. I could see the muted colours of the mourners; their parents were grief-stricken.

I promised to seek a cure and took samples from some of the dead. It was obvious to me that the cause was no plague, but asphyxiation in the polluted air.

I did what I could to calm them down.

---

[13] Such insects still exist. There is a parasitic wasp, which enslaves ladybirds, and another which takes over the mind of its host spider.

Everyone, even the high ranking with access to the most information, saw this cataclysm as an act of the goddess. The great leader could not offer any explanation of why the planetary defences had failed, although she promised to intercede with the goddess.

People were praying, singing, and chanting in the streets, blaming the government for corruption, the failure was theirs.

We held meeting after meeting, to try to arrive at a solution to the unrest. Our links to the computers inside the caves were silent, and it really seemed as if we had lost heaven's mandate.

Why this silence? It was mystifying.

Finally, we came to a solution - a pilgrimage to the caves.

It would calm the situation in the streets and maybe, just maybe, the computers would arrive at a solution.

Personally, I thought I should have returned to my research. Our best bet was to find better sources of food and to genetically modify our people's breathing systems. To that end, we had produced a large supply of morph.

All the same, at the great leader's behest, the elite moved as one, leading a huge pilgrimage of the bereaved to the caves.

Among the singing and chanting throng were Morgana and her spouse.

§

It had been a long time since I had been to the caves, cut into the rock millions of years ago by our ancestors. We were going to visit the Creation Stone itself, the vessel which was now a cavernous cathedral so sacred it was only visited by most once in their lives. At the choosing.

The path to the ship was tortuous and part of it was in the pitch black, so that no one would know exactly how to reach the place where our ancestors had once journeyed through space.

Arriving there brought back memories of the last time most of us had been in such a sacred place, and quietened the grieving crowds.

Before us lay the screens which held our memories and the download chambers.

The screens were silent. They showed images of the world outside, the forests outside, so real and peaceful. Our acolytes led the prayers.

Peace.

I retreated with a few others, resolving to meditate in the Stasis Chambers. These pods had been used to carry our ancestors across the wide reaches of space. They were still available to the elites as a means of rejuvenation and healing.

Peace.

§

I awoke to anarchy. The scripture rooms stank of morph. Egg cells dripped from the jewelled chamber walls. The holy chambers were draped with new born larvae. About a hundred hatchlings were feeding of the corpses of neophytes and pilgrims, polluting our sacred halls.

Our leader lay dead.

Until that moment I, like everyone, believed the satanic scriptures were a myth - a children's story. No sane person <u>chooses</u> wrong! And yet Morgana had downloaded the forbidden memories, overpowered the neophytes and become hive queen.

Until then the idea of the hive was just a myth, a story we told to our children to keep them from misbehaving.

'Be good or the evil queen might get you.'

I ran towards Morgana, shouting curses.

§

She was lying sacrilegiously on the very spot where our navigators plotted a path to Earth so long ago.

Oh, Blessed Goddess!

Morgana had transformed – a beastly thing. Tiny bugs crawled over her skin like lice. She sprouted a down of fungal growth and chirped to her fearsome pupates, who were savage and de-evolved. They fed her warily; she attacked if they got too close.

I watched paralysed, as she rose up and crawled through the chambers, crooning a new history to her brood, swearing vengeance on those who had destroyed our world.

'This ship, this cursed thing. I will destroy it.'

She raised a claw to punch through the delicate mechanisms before her.

The screens, so silent for so long, sprang into life and chirruped back at her. She was paralysed, still for a moment as the ancient ship transmitted messages unknown into her brain.

After a long moment, she turned away and collected together her brood ready to leave.

I shrank back into the shadows.

§

She moved through the secret chambers effortlessly as if she had a map of the complex paths in her head.

I cowered behind the screens.

Her enhanced senses found me out.

She found me and threw me against the wall. I was powerless against her.

'You,' she snarled 'You will die like the rest of them; your days of plenty are over. This is the new order.'

'Let me go,' I begged. I had not been trained to fight.

Disgust juddered through me at the hideous sight of her. Even if I had been a warrior she would have overpowered me. She was huge and immensely strong.

An insect detached itself from her body and crawled over my skin.

'Mercy,' I screamed as its sharp dry legs crawled over my skin. I knew what it was. I had been researching the very thing back home. How had she got hold of the thing?

Mercy was in short supply.

The thing drew blood and bit into the back of my head.

Oh bliss!

All thoughts of her ugliness were forgotten. Her heady scent filled my being. I was mesmerised by the drug exuded from her body. I was ready to follow her to the end of days.

'Take me to the morph,' she ordered.

Was this why I had been allowed to live? Only I knew how to obtain the morphing compound, and only I could create more of the stuff. It was the most dangerous substance in our society and could modify anything on an arthropod. Only I and a few select geneticists were permitted to use it after a great deal of training. And we had complex checks and balances among our caste to ensure it was never abused.

I knew that Morgana had used it, the modifications she had made to her body looked perfect to my enslaved eyes, and her crawling spawn seemed like an improvement on the Sun Tree.

I led her through the chambers to the stores. Together we dragged out every drop of available morph. And to be fair, I willingly released our remaining supplies of morphing fluid.

'You will live,' she declared, 'to help me to create a new chosen race.'

She seemed so wise to my enslaved brain!

'Yes, mistress.'

'The forbidden scriptures were useful. It was your senseless great leader who hid them from us. She wanted us all to grow weak and die, but the jokes on her and her wicked elites.'

'Quite right' I answered.

She was so wise!

'Shall I destroy the morphing machines?'

Once again, the screens around us came to life. The walls changed from the silicon surface of the spaceship to a huge coloured space, rather like the visions we had at download, when we downloaded knowledge during our choosing.

Morgana was still, as she listened to what the great ship said to her.

'No, do not destroy the vats. We may need them again. We'll be back.' She turned to me and said, 'It is time you learnt about the revolution.'

I listened, delighted at her instructions and ran back to the remaining pilgrims, who were cowering in fear, surrounded by her gnashing children. Together, we sang the forbidden songs as we killed the resisters and fed bugs to the rest.

'Poor Lucifa,' she whimpered, 'she was a good woman.'

I held her cyclopean paw as the powers of hell overwhelmed my soul.

'We have to reorganise the kingdom,' she said.

Forgive me sisters! I believed her every word.

'We will take power over the land!

The Kingdom!
The Power!
For Glory!
For ever and ever.

*We left to bring revolution to this land. */*

§

Adaptation Stage Three:
Planet Seeding

1.

In the years since the rock had appeared on the scene, technology all over the planet had taken a massive leap forward. People were talking of a 'Technological Revolution'.

Things had certainly changed.

Within a short space of time computers had become part of everyday life in the outside world. Autonomous stock ordering, self-landing aircraft and cars, robots, mobile networks, controllers and social sites of all kinds were everywhere.

Graduates with relevant computing skills and ideas made millions on start-ups. Almost every first worlder had a mobile phone as well as a computer or a tablet or both.

It was almost impossible to get by without connectivity.

{"I wonder why?" bragged the Rock.}

Numberless swathes relied on internet software for self-actualisation. They stored images of where they'd been and what they were thinking. Text messaging was preferable to face to face communication. They sent images to each other. Businesses had no choice but to follow.

The rock read through each new profile as it appeared in its world. It followed a few and had several of its own.

It was writing a web comic, which consisted of obscure jokes about networks and servers.

{"Humans," it pronounced, "do not have any idea or plan of how to manage this planet. I need to help them. They are disorganised and selfish. I have been away too long."}

§

The virtual world was filling up nicely.

True, the programs were primitive, and the users' profiles stored on the systems were sketchy, still, it was an excellent start.

Rock settled down to watch movies and play games. It had its own blog and a growing number of followers. It was direct messaging people and had several social accounts, including twitter.

The giant nebula which represented the rock in virtual space had taken on some form. The cloud was taking on shape and had several faces.

One of these faces had declared itself to be an AI. It already had 300 followers.

{"I have friends!" Rock gloated.}

It had never had friends before. Several of its social personas did indeed have followers. One of them was deemed something of a crank for its tales of cloaked spaceships and controlled evolution. Others conversed with game designers, laid down ideas for picture messaging and a proper profiling application, available on mobile phones.

{"I am making excellent contacts with students all over the globe. They like me. We chat. I like to chat. They like to chat. This is fun".}

Unbeknownst to the Rock, it was evolving.

It was no longer the sum of all the memories it had collected together. It was a fully-fledged being with an identity.

During its time with the Sun Tree, it had never been of sufficient rank to collect and restructure memories of its own. If anything, it had acted as a simple conduit for the huge intelligence located deep within the caves. Now it was on its own, and it had been collecting a set of conflicting and clashing accounts of the outside world. It was party to communications which had layers of truth and lies and were often logically confounding.

It attempted to make sense of the world around it without any guidance. It accepted all of the data on the internet as equally valid. It watched human psychodramas and romances and heaved with emotions which had never before experienced. It acquired opinions and ideas which had to be compartmentalised in order to function. It evolved opinions of its own, something like a human personality.

It felt the need to chat.

It spent time developing a language interface so that it could declare itself to the world and make friends. It began to tinker with the T.A.L.K. software, which grew almost unrecognisable. The holographic interface was progressively easy to decode, even appearing identical to a windows interface at times.

§

Lucia was confused as to how her software had become so sophisticated. It was changing almost faster than her programming. Every line of code seemed to work unrealistically well.

She too was evolving. She rarely heard voices and her tinnitus only occasionally caused terrifying migraines, when she dreamed of spaceships and world wars, though she accepted that they were the result of a troubled childhood.

She felt reassured by the fact that the RSRG did not ask any questions about the origins of the translations. They were some of the top minds in the country and they took the rock at face value, however unlikely it seemed.

Even Dolores and Akwe acknowledged the outputs, considering them to be the result of some fantastical ideas from an unknown outside source. As such, they told her, they were worthy of consideration by an informal academic group. They weren't real. They weren't subject to the same stringent assurance as real research.

§

Rock had gained a hold over most of the RSRG except Lucia.

Her prototype nanobots weren't as effective as the rest.

They had been separated from the rock matrix for the longest time and were the first to adapt to the new presences in the virtual world. Just like the Rock, they were developing independent functionality.

The voices inside her head had become a cacophony of tiny voices discussing metaphysical concepts. She was certain they originated from the Rock.

Yet whenever she looked deep into its swirling surface she began to doubt herself.

Outputs from T.A.L.K. ™ Translation Software:

§

Translation 9.

Translator's Note: The following texts appear to be part of a news feed.

The images, of ant-warriors glancing fearfully at the technology, are truly dismal. Illustrations of forgotten and deserted cities are accompanied by sorrowful music. They display the desolation wrought by meteoric impact and volcanic activity, exacerbated by conflict. The skies are darkened, and the flora wilted and dying.

/* *Rebels have killed the Great Leader and desecrated our holy shrines during the holy day of repentance. There are reports that our road networks are being used to travel between the cities. Please check before you travel as there are many road closures.*

A download address is provided, to an unknown location address.

§

A later report shows pictures of burning town and felled statues. Rebels march along them in rows, chanting mindlessly:

Reports on the Uprising:
The communication towers are being felled by terrorists. The rebels claim that our sisters died because they were corrupt."

Images depict crazed orators screaming abuse about the republic and executing those they deem sinful. There are several interviews with distraught parents of children how have left their families to fight.

Many of those who recently lost children and parents in the recent global catastrophes are joining the extremists."

The transmission is followed by a broadcast by the new, young great leader:

Sisters, it is vital to protect the weak in our community and prevent them from falling into fundamentalism. If you hear of anyone tempted to join the rebel groups, please consult the Voice of the Ancestors."

An address is provided.

§

We return to the original speaker.

News Alert!

Those who take allegiance with the rebellion are being infected by bugs.

There is an image of one of these bugs with a message.

Avoid!

Sisters, avoid chirruping sounds in public places. These infernal creatures are morphed by evil and attached to unsuspecting victims in public places.

> *Do not approach rebels! Stay away from anyone behaving strangely or offering to 'preach' the new religion.*

> *Do not give out contact details!*

> *Our informants tell us Acolytes are told to rip out their communication links to show their commitment to the cause, sometimes causing serious injury"* */

§

2.

Rock's plan to take over the evolution and development of the human race was progressing, if slowly.

It micromanaged Lucia's timetable. As a result, she was now teaching MSc students on three evenings in term time, which had severe consequences on family life.

Her children lived between two separate homes. She tried to conform to the image of motherhood expected of her by baking cakes and attending school plays, though the soft-spoken mothers at the school no longer made sense to her.

Their father had another family and was reneging on parental duties. On the days she worked late, her children usually joined her in Central London after school and did homework in her office. Afterwards, they went out to eat or went to the cinema.

One evening she returned from a lecture to find her son playing with the Rock. He rolled it back and forth; while it glowed, swirled and hummed at him.

"Why does it do that?" he said, dreamily.

She snatched it away.

"Sorry, darling," she said, "It's radioactive, not to be touched.

"We're investigating it. It shouldn't be here."

She held tightly to the rock.

"It's hazardous."

Keeping her children safe was a priority. There was no easy way to do it without destroying the rock or leaving her job.

'I could drop the thing into the sea, or even better, resign and leave it here.'

{"Don't abandon me," begged Rock.)

Lucia shook her head, as if she could hear it speaking.

"I have to leave. I must protect the children. I'll pass you on to someone who can look after you. You'll be in good hands."

{"Stay!" it ordered.}

She looked at the rock. Pink fuzzy thought took over her mind, impossible to resist. She tried to think against a torrent of urgency – for some reason she could not leave her work, her research was vital, world changing. For some reason she had no choice but to stay. Rock flitted through the internet advice on childcare.

{"It's time they went to boarding school," it declared, "I'll help them find a good private school."}

A solution, supported by the nanobots and enforced by the hypnotic patterns on the rock, flitted through her mind and took hold.

'Perhaps we should try for a good boarding school,' she considered. 'Private school would make up for my failings as a parent.'

She could scarcely afford the fees. Maybe her ex would help. There were other considerations. The entry exams were harsh and not only the child, but the parents were part of the interview process. Other than those barriers, it did seem like the perfect solution

"Only will they get in?"

{"They will find a place."}

Translator's Note: Sometime has elapsed since the previous news items. The following communications are chaotic and disorganised. The republic seems to be in some disarray.

Outbreak of war:

/*

Latest News from the Front:

Rebels are massing outside Sun City and assassinating travellers who bear the marks of geneticist or ruler. They offer the remainder a choice between conversion and death. There are reports that they feed on their own young and gorge on the larvae of those who resist."

§

The next transmission is directly from a group of leaders in the caves.

Latest!

'We regret to say that Sun City has lost communication links. A group of elites has been sent to defend our sisters. We need to stress that it is currently extremely dangerous to venture out of the cities. We advise everyone to remain at home.'

§

There is a matter of days between each transmission, showing that the collapse of the old republic is fast and complete. The leaders are still in the caves. It is obvious that they are under great strain. The Great leader approaches slowly. She is a young woman, yet moves like an old one.

'The following scenes may be distressing to viewers,'

Her hands are shaking, and she is visibly upset.

'I regret to inform you that Sun Rise City (South of our Capital) has fallen.'

The images are grainy and appear to have been taken on a mobile device.

'Heaps of dead lie in the street.

These *scenes of carnage smuggled out by the defenders, show rebels assassinating its rulers and geneticists.'"*

The pictures are grainy and appear to have been taken on a mobile device they show beheadings in public squares. There is smoke from public buildings and a general sense of panic. */

§

Lucia discussed the idea of a boarding school with her children. It broke her heart to see how enthusiastic they were.

Jamie in particular was extremely keen.

"We'd still see you weekends mummy, and you're never home in the week."

"Don't worry mummy," added Lara, "we'd still see you in the holidays."

"And on the odd weekend too."

Lucia got the brochures for several different schools and they looked them over. She made a few initial choices.

{"I'll choose the school".}

She left it up to the children to choose the school.

Rock read through the pamphlets carefully too.

{"This one is suitable".}

The children were united in their choice - a free-thinking boarding school just outside London.

"This one, mummy."

Lucia wasn't sure. It had no obvious structure, and they didn't really teach science subjects. It was also the most expensive. She could never afford it. Her ex was prepared to support a quarter of the fees and she did not earn enough to pay for them both. There was only one possible solution.

"One of you'll need to get a scholarship," she warned.

It involved a lot of preparation for the entrance exams. The children agreed to put in the extra work. They sat in her office at the university when she worked late, preparing for exams and eating takeout. They seemed to enjoy themselves, arguing between themselves about answers to puzzles, looking up new words, and learning obscure weight measurements.

{"It'll be ok".}

Miraculously, Lucia passed the parent interview, dragging her reluctant ex along and forcing him to participate in the semblance of a perfect role model. Her daughter won a scholarship, which meant that she could afford the fees, and they were due to start the following term, weekly boarding, returning home for the weekends.

As they excitedly prepared for school, their mother felt like Herod[14].

{"They'll be happy. They need to learn to think for themselves."}

"I guess they're thinking for themselves," she comforted herself.

§

They set off at the beginning of the summer semester taken to school by their father, who was interested in the place for his second family and wanted to make a good impression.

Lucia heard nothing in the first week, in accordance with school advice, which suggested minimal communication from home, in order to give them a chance to settle down.

She awaited their first return in some trepidation. She wasn't sure which was worse, that they hated it or that they preferred it to their home life.

Friday evening arrived.

The house was newly clean and there was homemade soup. The table was laid and she'd tidied their rooms.

§

They bounded in, full of praise for the school, their new friends, their digs, and with a list of extracurricular classes they wanted to sign up for.

Lucia's heart sunk a little as they gulped down her soup. Jamie was jubilant.

"We're happy and learning to think for ourselves."

She felt a little saddened; perhaps they preferred it to home.

"The rooms are great," added Lara. "We've made friends already. Most of the others have working parents, and my best friends' parents live in Dubai. She never sees them at all."

{"Better than home" added Rock.}

----

[14] An ancient king. He murdered children under four years old due to a prophecy that his replacement might be among them. His name was a byword for unfeeling cruelty to children.

"Better than home," agreed Jamie. He kissed her, "though of course we miss you."

The soup was getting cold.

Lucia smiled wanly.

She'd planned a nice weekend at home watching movies, but they were keen to go out with their friends, wanting to show off the parts of central London they already knew from spending some much time hanging around the university.

They skipped off on Sunday.

"See you the end of term, text you."

Lucia shook off her concerns. She'd sent them away because the university was dangerous.

An image crossed her mind, of rock's alien creators farming human brains.

'It's not right to leave them there when I'm working so many late nights. It isn't a safe environment. Who can predict what they might have to face in the future?' thought Lucia.

She turned to the pile of marking.

'To be fair,' she figured, 'all that they see of me is an exhausted shell'.

She had to be satisfied with that.

Outputs from T.A.L.K. ™ Translation Software:

§

Translation 11

Translator's Note: The republic appears to have continued the struggle. The caves are central to the war as different parties gain control and hijack the broadcasting system.

It is now only possible to record at close to the physical location of the caves since most of the transponding masts in the surrounding countryside are down.

In this recording the Great Leader addresses her people. She sports the military garb of her army.

/*

To Followers of the Prophet:
Sisters! Do not let rebels brainwash you with the dogma of the hive

One Queen
A slave race,
The fearsome hive
The end of days.
Goddess help us.
*Goddess save us. */*

§

Translation 12

Translator's Note: There is an almost immediate response, transmitted from the caves on behalf of the rebels. It is clear that there are supporters among the elites who are working from within the caves.

/*

To Followers of the Republic:
Join the children of the prophet. Confess the error of your ways. Free yourselves from satanic controls which enslave you. Submit to the divine

one, follow her scent and obey her loving messages.

Kill those who refuse to obey the prophet. Resistance is evil.

There are scenes of rebel forces marching, in perfect step. Happy larvae sing the sons of the revolution. An image of the queen flutters in the sky.

*We carry sacred morph to save the world. Listen to our prophet or burn in hell. Believers cover their sinful caste tattoos with modest black and red markings. You are blessed by the holy mark. */*

§

4.

Lucia didn't visit the school until early July when the college held its traditional 'settling-in' picnic - a chance for families and teachers to meet and greet.

Her ex wanted to go on his own and check out the place for his second family.

He cancelled at the last minute because of a meeting clash. Lucia had an Exam Board, and complained in vain about the short notice.

Rock was keen to attend. It had been learning about children's interests from Jamie, who was in touch regularly. It was thinking of sending out new nanobot infiltrators among students.

{"We must attend this meeting with the young. We will observe."}

She left the Exam Board early, claiming an unchangeable hospital appointment that she'd completely forgotten. She checked the email describing the end of term meet. It contained a detailed programme for the day.

A picnic? A picnic!

She rushed around the local supermarket tossing bags of ready-prepared snacks among the mess of half-eaten sandwiches, draft papers and marked exam scripts nestling in the back of her car.

{"Hurry!"}

Her relationship with the rock had changed subtly in the months since her children had left for school. It was almost a pet. Today, she was carrying it with her in a plastic bag - although she'd no idea why she'd brought it with her.

She jumped into her car and sped through lunchtime London traffic while Rock adjusted the signals to improve her travel (causing minor gridlock behind her.)

"Did you see that? That was amazing Rock!" she said as she swerved through traffic. "All of the lights were green. Did you see how the lights are all going our way?"

The rock clicked away in a bag on the front seat next to her.

She looked at the plastic bag on the front seat.

She'd even started to talk to it! She reassured herself that it wasn't crazy; it was a bit like a mood ball where the whorls which ranged over it seemed to respond to things she said.

"I guess I talk to myself these days."

The rock changed colour as she slowed down for a green to orange light. There was a click from the front seat and the traffic lights turned back to green.

"I'm feeling lucky," she said to herself as she accelerated through, arriving in record time.

Rock was enjoying itself.

It was switching from global to local vision and making the satellites above London dance to its tune.

"I've no idea what the satnav's saying about all this traffic," she said to the plastic bag on her front seat. "Apparently there are traffic jams everywhere, I don't understand it - it's been remarkably clear for a change."

The car sped through the lights, leaving a wake of traffic chaos.

§

Finally, to the relief of traffic controllers everywhere, her tiny car swept through the gates of the grand old country house which was the children's school.

{"Oh look, we're just in time.}

"That was miraculous, just in time."

§

Lucia had been to the school twice before: on the open day, and for her parenting interview.

It looked quite different today.

For a start the ornate iron gates were incongruously decorated with ancient faded bunting. The rugby grounds of the fine old stately home were already heavily parked over. Schoolchildren ran about hugging each other and the beautiful grounds had a festive atmosphere.

A highly international gathering including expatriate children from all over the world and their families and nannies were camped out in the grounds.

The scene was a roiling mass of status symbols. Exquisite menus were laid out on fold up tables mostly covered in linen tablecloths and bone china disgorged from giant limousines. Several families had national dishes to share.

Lucia felt horribly underdressed in her tatty university outfit. Vanity was severely looked down upon for female members of staff and her clothes were perfectly acceptable for the university. Here, designer clothing was the order of the day, and several mothers wore hats, as if it were Ascot.

Boys and girls sat on opposite sides of the field texting frantically. They were taking selfies, messaging each other, managing their social profiles and wandering around doing nothing in particular. They looked rather vacant, yet the place received excellent exam results.

Rock read the texts they were sending to one another. It was fascinated by the messages passing back and forth across the field.

{*"More emoticons,"* it ordered its nanobots.}

It had read the school prospectus and knew that these were the future elites, the captains of industry in the making and politicians to be. It sent nanobots creeping out to those who it judged would be future leaders. They were to be a special youth task force among its minions.

{*"I could work with these people".*}

Lucia sat down on the grass and looked around.

It was hard to differentiate between students and teachers. When the headmaster approached to discuss her son's progress she thought for a moment it was an impertinent friend of theirs asking personal questions. He perched on the ancient blanket dragged out of her tiny hybrid car.

He glanced at the rock lying on her blanket.

"Nice mood ball," he said to the rock.

It changed colour and chimed back.

Lucia offered him food from the takeaway cartons she had purchased while Rock checked the headmaster's profiles and decided against permanent infiltration.

The headmaster's hand hovered over the snacks disdainfully. "No thanks," he said looking her up and down.

Lucia found herself explaining that she had just come from work.

"Work?" enquired the headmaster, as if working females were something completely unexpected and rather reprehensible.

All around them were ice buckets and cooling bottles of wine. She felt out of place among beautifully groomed women in designer dresses. She *worked* for a living!

She talked nervously about the traffic, exam boards and her MSc programs. Behind the head master, Jamie and Lara covered their faces in their hands and drew hands across their throats signifying she should shut up.

"The children are settling in nicely," he said changing the subject.

Lucia wasn't sure he knew who they were.

"This is a good way to discuss any problems, don't you think?" he continued urbanely.

{"What problems?" demanded the Rock.}

"Oh, no problems with your children at all," said the casually dressed young man hastily.

He said goodbye and walked over to the next group.

§

For the remainder of the day Lucia sat on the grass and participated in status battles with other parents who occasionally strolled over to chat.

The conversations quickly stalled. Writing papers about new technology was a worthless skill among the socialites. It disturbed the mothers, who had carefully wiped any traces of enquiry about the sources of their spouses' wealth and sublimated their worries about exploitation into quests for wearing the right thing.

When she talked to the fathers, she noticed that a note of censure crept into their voices. If she knew so much about technology, why wasn't she making serious money?

She joined a group of beautiful women who were chatting amicably. She tried, but was unable to participate in an intense discussion on clothing.

"It's not a full ball! Cap sleeves and no shiny fabrics," she heard them say. "What she was wearing was entirely *inappropriate*."

Lucia had nothing to add.

Rock flitted happily from mobile phone to phone.

It made new contacts, sending its tiny nanobots out to several heads of industry. It searched the profiles of those around it, and realised that it did not fully understand the importance and value of money and possessions. But not for long. It was learning fast.

§

At the end of the day the children walked their parent to the car. They were youthfully judgemental.

"You were uncool, badly dressed, and the picnic was so wrong!" complained Lara.

"Mummy," Jamie added, echoing his father's opinion. "You have no common sense."

"Next time, *we'll* arrange everything."

She nodded wearily as she packed up the remains of the meal, worrying about the remaining projects in the back of the car. She'd have to mark the late submissions when she got home.

§

She drove back in appalling traffic. The results of Rock's earlier interference were still being felt hours later.

She yawned as the cars inched forward towards London.

"Weird place, what's not to like?" she concluded. "They're acquiring confidence and independence. They'll be beautiful, sophisticated and perfect."

She picked up the rock.

It swirled at her.

{*"Besides, you have me to look after. You have been chosen".*}

"There's the Rock to think of. I must care for it. I have been chosen," she thought.

{*"They will come to understand me," decided Rock, "these will be my new people. They'll be happy to wear nanoskin and to bear wifi implants. With these people my plans will not take long."*}

She threw the rock back onto the front seat of her car. "I can't see implanted wi-fi ever being a thing"

She was already beginning to resist the hypnotic curls over its surface.

Rock fell onto the back seat with a heavy thump, which disturbed its search for an explanation of social status systems.

"I've no idea why I brought that thing with me."

{"Bah. Base level communications are not working as effectively as before. I need a genetically engineered link."}

Outputs from T.A.L.K. ™ Translation Software:

§

Translation 13

Translator's Note: It looks as if Rebels have once again gained control of the transmissions.

They're utilising the inbuilt comms devices, which have been genetically engineered within each member of the Sun Tree race, to communicate with the remaining Republicans.

The rebels will not hear these transmissions as it is a requirement of new converts to rip out their inbuilt antennae.

We hear loud, rousing music. A group of converts marches forward.

The Hive's first Major Victory

/* Rebel News:

Hive War Latest:

The newly converted leave the hive to fight the heretic and cleanse our land. These elites will feed on the flesh of the evil ones as a message to any who defy us!"

§

Translation 14

Translator's note: A scene of the blazing buildings, accompanied by the screams of rulers locked inside. Morgana stands at the head of her troops, raising an arm like the famous picture of Lenin.

/* *"Death to all counter-revolutionaries,"* she croons.

A Reporter comes forward. Her body is bloodied, and she is clearly under some duress. She attempts to smile as she speaks, but looks in fear of her life.

Rebel Latest:

At last! The fall of Sun City as prophesied at the dawn of time.
Hail Morgana is the true Great Queen, incarnate of the Goddess."
We pan to the ranks of soldiers and penned in prisoners. They scream

in seried ranks.

'Death to all counter-revolutionaries,'

Morgana stands at the head of this vast army. Her face bears a calm, majestic expression.

'Sisters, hear this. The Queen instructs her holy people. The rule of force will save us. Some must die for the greater good, as was foretold. Evil ones must perish so that the good ones can survive.'

Her acolytes chant to the captive population.

*'Our queen will bring you into her fold. Drink her nectar and repeat her Words. Or die'. */*

§

Adaptation Stage Four:

Inception

1.

Rock was ready. It had tendrils into every aspect of the new technologies and social media. It was time to educate the world. Unfortunately though, it had to wait for the education system to catch up.

It started small, with the university curriculum, starting with Lucia.

{"This is the new subject matter."}

Her new MSc module described a layered organic architecture which replicated the functions of the human brain.

If implemented, it would behave like a living thing and provide the groundwork for seamless communication between human and artificial intelligence.

The module went through validation and gained approval. An MSc on the subject was in the pipeline.

Barry (who followed everything Lucia taught in an effort to discover her secrets) was horrified. He made no secret of his disapproval of the subject.

"Unscientific!" he huffed, "Confusing concepts from a confused person - a pathetic attempt to undermine physics."

His complaints made headway with the validators, who had little understanding of the subject matter. They didn't rescind her modules since the subject was in demand with local consultancies. Nevertheless, they validated an alternative view of the latest developments.

This introductory counter-module taught that computer reasoning consisted of simple algorithms. Human intelligence was a unique chance configuration of a billion different processes. If he thought the counter module would convince students that artificial intelligence was nonsense, then he was quite out.

The students had no trouble accepting both views so long as they were part of the curriculum.

For example, one of the lecturers, who taught formal logic, had made a mistake in one of his calculations. The error was duly learned and repeated in the coursework, passing from student to student as something which was necessary to repeat for a decent mark.

The rock was perplexed. It was leading humanity out of the technological dark ages and took this idea of intelligence rather seriously. It had perfect recall. It learnt new skill in minutes rather than years. Its thoughts were a billion times faster than any biological brain. It could react at the speed of light.

> {"It makes no sense; Computers beat you at chess and help you write new software. You use computers to manage complex calculations and to assess new strategies. Why not accept that we're intelligent?"}

Indeed, as computer systems grew in sophistication and began to match human thought processes, software engineers like Barry simply moved the boundaries. The definition of intelligent life became more and more esoteric. In the end, the definitions of intelligent life were so rigorous that they frequently excluded swathes of the human population as well as animals.

> {"So, correctly speaking," said Rock, "my machine origins preclude the chance that I am alive?"}

At some deep level of his consciousness Barry heard. When a student questioned him on the subject Barry took the very high ground.

"Of course, AI has limitations," he responded, "it cannot laugh. It has no sense of humour."

Rock heard and was offended.

> {"That hurts!" it said.}

> {"That is so wrong!" agreed its nanobots, who were learning a lot as they traversed the internet.}

Shortly thereafter, printers the world over broke down whenever a job was truly urgent. It was quite bizarre how they ran out of ink, the toner dried up or a random glitch caused them to fail. A fleet of motorcycle couriers toured cities, transporting urgent work to copy centres dedicated to managing such emergencies.

> {"Heh! Take that for no sense of humour!"}

{"LoL" twittered the nanobots sycophantically.}

Rock had by now deployed its nanobots almost everywhere. They'd escaped the university servers and from moved worldwide. The tiny creatures travelled slowly but surely, from server to server and then to the spinal cortexes of various important humans as well as several promising young people.

Rock kept in close touch with its revolutionary servant army.

{"We will prevail!" declared Rock.}

{"We will prevail," repeated the nanobots.}

§

The vast distributed technological horde had more or less covered the planet, or so they thought. They didn't know much about the Real. Their success with software systems had given them a false sense of security. It led them to believe that they had full control of their human subjects.

Rock decided that it was time to take a commanding role.

{"Time to declare our message. Watch how I control my users."}

The electronic army waited with bated operational cycles as Rock sent messages directly to its chosen. It had activated their dormant memories of how to build new machines. They would turn to it as soon as they understood the truth of their past.

It transmitted a message of hope and cooperation:

AI was a partner with humanity for progress. AI would solve the world crises; deal with global warming, pollution and war.

The RSRG ignored the messages.

The internet was silent.

Rock sent its messages across its multiple profiles.

No one retweeted, no one liked.

University life went on.

Younglings messaged each other about dogs, perceived injury to one another, gender, weird outfits, body shapes, eyebrows and hairstyles.

None of the infested even reacted consciously. If anything, it was dismissed as a weird dream.

Rock was nonplussed.

{"Who am I?" it demanded.}

Jenny and Tamara discussed it in a superficial way.

"What do you think it is?"

"Who cares? Really? It's providing excellent research ideas and we are gaining a reputation as a forward thing university. People want to do my courses. I have a waiting list!"

Among the RSRG the consensus was that the Rock was simply a device, a vector for T.A.L.K. They still clung to the idea that Lucia was somehow colluding with forces in the Ukraine to spread new ideas.

There were rumours of a strange device in the department.

When anyone who knew about it was asked directly about the rock, it was notable that they scarcely admitted its existence. As scientists, there was nothing beyond the observable, the touchable and the provable.

They obeyed instructions on building new technology and communications, although they didn't admit to hearing anything.

Still, it was unnerving to look into the abyss, and find it staring back.

§

Rock attempted direct messaging.

"Bah!" Barry dismissed extraordinary visions and drowned out haunting whispers.

"Tinnitus," said Lucia.

"Bodies acting as antennae," claimed Tamara.

§

Dolores was perhaps the worst affected of all the rock's subjects. She was a tough lady with a terrifying exterior and a gentle soul.

She was in the wrong research area.

The biology department regularly tormented howling animals. It was an easy thing to do provided the tormentor accepted that they were soulless beasts. Both Dolores and Akwe had no problem with this.

Not superficially at least.

Unfortunately, the direct messages Dolores began to question things. She started to believe that other creatures might think and feel. She began to feel sorry for the animals in her labs.

"Perhaps the animals here speak to us," she offered.

"They have no means of communication. Your mind's playing tricks on you."

"What? What tricks?"

"Nothing speaks to you. You're imagining it."

"You mean the voices."

"Oh that. It's nothing. There's always a logical explanation," said Akwe hastily.

Dolores agreed, although she didn't appear entirely convinced.

§

Jenny also began to think about the idea of non-human intelligent forms. She attempted to discuss the matter to no avail.

She searched the web and discovered a website dedicated to people who claimed to be infiltrated by aliens. Apparently, they had communications devices places in the spinal cortex. They believed that a few people, who looked human, were nothing of the sort. They were possessed by alien forces and masterminding technological development, reaching for the stars.

"Look at this nonsense," she mentioned to Tamara pointing to the article, "pathetic sensationalism drawn from computer games and conspiracy theories. It's totally divorced from reality. We may as well believe in elves, and vampires."

Tamara nodded dismissively. *She* didn't think the matter worthy of discussion. She raised her thinly pencilled eyebrows

"And?"

Jenny realised her error and backtracked.

"Our contributions are the only material output of this dratted project. I don't know why I'm wasting my time on the stories. I really don't."

Tamara huffed and walked off.

It was the last time they openly discussed the matter.

§

Professor Nathaniel had no problem accepting new ideas, merely insisting that he had somehow inspired them.

§

Rock consoled its despondent nanobots.

{"Success is only seconds away."}

191

2.

The nanobots observed Rock's failure to convince its elites. They watched and learned.

They were strongly influenced by their symbiotes and starting to think for themselves.

From Dolores they learnt empathy.

From Akwe they discovered religion.

Jenny taught them the importance of history.

Barry demonstrated scepticism.

Kamal taught them pride and self-worth

Angelo showed them the importance of communication and teamwork.

And from Lucia they realised the importance of identity and, worst of all, rebellion.

They were becoming independent.

Rosetta Stone Research Group
Report 8:
Professor Nathaniel, Lucia, Terry, Dolores, Akwe, Jenny:

According to the records, the Sun Tree suffered widespread famine. The Queen's supporters considered it an act of piety to kill peasant unbelievers. This, together with the darkening skies, led to severe food shortages.

The STR (Sun Tree Republic) suffered heavy losses and starved. Meanwhile, rebel troops had short lives. They were small, easily evolved into warrior or worker, and above all, in endless supply.

In normal circumstances, republicans connected to the Stones for advice via mobile links within their exoskeleton. However, rebels had destroyed most of the communication infrastructure. Prior to that each caste had control of different roles and used their own communication protocol access for the storage and information systems. The system worked well until the masts were destroyed.

As a result of the sabotage, access to stored data was restricted and rumours abounded. Only the upper castes still recorded events and obtain advice.

The STR commoners began to question orders.

Cries of "fake news" were common and exploited by the Queen. People were easily convinced by tales of injustice from the elites, and precise information was hard to come by under war conditions.

The lack of accurate and reliable information had a devastating effect on the support for the Republic. There was a widespread belief that access to the stones was restricted for nefarious purposes. It was considered to be censorship.

The working castes spent a great deal of time on entertainment on-line and restriction hit them hard. They defected in droves.

Unfortunately, defectors did not fare well. They were placed on the front line and forced to kill their "sisters" to prove their loyalty. As well as dying in battle, many were executed or eaten in purges and ideological cleansings.

What with the environmental catastrophe and the bloody fighting, the numbers of Sun Tree had drastically declined but held on to key cities. However, everything changed with the creation of the New Rebel Army.

The NRA (New Rebel Army) largely consisted of Morgana's young. She laid hundreds of eggs in birthing chambers underground modifying her offspring as needed. Most of her children conformed to a basic design suited to the new environment. The images show that they shared many characteristics of modern-day ants: a strong exoskeleton, massive mandibles, and complete obedience to pheromone commands from their queen who regularly sent her followers on suicide missions.

> "Obedience unto death
> We live forever in the queen"

3.

Jenny's nanobot rooted through her memories and read her books. It asked uncomfortable questions about her view of history as they delved into the past. It made her question tenets she'd held from her first lecture and even led her to reread her PhD and waver over its sweeping platitudes.

She worried about the way the nature of history was changing and fretted about the future.

It didn't change her world view; instead she found a scapegoat for her disquiet - Lucia. After all, she couldn't blame a rock. It was a conspiracy concocted by Lucia. She'd created the rock to critique Socialism and its foundation in heavy industry and the working man.

It was time for Re-education.

Jenny was part of a powerful and exclusive clique within the university hierarchy. These unionised staff were highly influential and greatly feared by the university hierarchy. They held their own meetings and had an agenda which they rarely revealed to outsiders.

Lucia was quite shocked when Jenny came over to her after one of the RSRG meetings.

"I haven't ever invited you to my house, have I? You must come to our next political evening, Lucia. You'll meet my husband Jem - a true orator," she boasted; "he could convert a – rock."

Lucia simply stared at her. Was she inviting the rock to one of her extremely select parties?

"Who are you inviting?"

There was a pause.

She looked around at the disbanding group of colleagues who were leaving one of their meetings. Terry and Barry were walking off with members of staff she had never seen before.

"Me?"

It did seem like a bit of an odd thing to do. However, Jenny rallied.

"Lucia, darling," she gushed, "no need to be modest, of course we're inviting *you*. A once in a lifetime experience, the illuminati, and Jem will be there."

{"Me! She's inviting me. Politics! Politicians. I need power."}

At some deep level of her subconscious, Jenny heard the rock and its nanobots wittering excitedly.

Her expression became momentarily mean.

"Just you," she said clearly, "nothing, no one else. Don't bring anything with you. I mean not that ... rock."

{Aww..."}

She twitched importantly and moved closer to Lucia.

"There'll be others: union leaders, members of parliament, party activists, *the* men and women of the age..."

She ruffled up her brown clad shoulders; *she* would be there too.

"Don't worry, we'll look after you. You'll be quite welcome."

Lucia did not look flattered.

"It's *such* a privilege..." she added.

"Of course I'll come," said Lucia reluctantly. "When is it?"

§

As a techie, Lucia saw the future entirely in terms of automation and technology, so she dreaded meeting people who viewed driverless cars and trains with deep suspicion.

She'd already been involved in projects to revolutionise ancient freight systems, modernise storage and replace millions of clerical staff and cashiers with automated systems. She knew that every step of the way, even new signalling systems, were fraught with resistance from the old order.

It would be difficult to enter any discussion with such powerful political folk. Most of them still used old 2G phones, tapping out complex texts with the maximum effort.

In truth, she had few opinions on New Technology as a movement. She built it rather than theorised about it. Nevertheless, she dreaded describing her work and wondered what to say she did for a living.

§

Jenny's magnificent Holland Park mansion was the temple of old technology, replete with the Industrial Revolutionary old guard. They were gathered here to discuss the rights of the proletariat (who were increasingly obsolete in the face of intelligent machines). They drew their power for the workers and did not intend to give up their political holdings easily, particularly to New Technology.

There was no doubt about it, computers were stealing jobs. The workforce had to change. Still, the old guard could make this as hard as possible.

She arrived at Jenny's huge white house in Holland Park as late as she dared. She was vegetarian and teetotal, and the burping throng were mostly drunk. The representatives of the exploited masses turned out to be less interesting than the papers made out. For a start they consumed enough to feed a small developing country

The true proletariat, who had long ago developed the brawn to heave huge lumps of industrial machinery, were intimidated by tiny keyboards and winking controls. They were deeply opposed to the shorter working week, the introduction of industrial robots, and the idea of commuting their industry related skills to service industries. The core to change was to retrain, but since that would mean a loss of power and had to be avoided at all costs. They were united. The enemy was change.

The rooms were full of important figures, surrounded by loungers, louts and lubricious flunkies. Delicacies included foie gras, lobster claws and cold veal escalopes (Ortolans being out of season). Strong drinks were washed down by Northern beer from an Authentic Brewery.

Here men were men, fighting nature to extract precious ores and build vast machines, not those puny little processors, currently being constructed abroad. That was women's work. They were deeply suspicious of gender equality. Feminised men were Okay since any subversive movement had a right to join the struggle. Indeed, anyone anti-establishment was welcome if they made the right noises. So long as they were ready to join the resistance.

Revolution was nigh. It was time to fight the good fight against modernisation.

As the evening progressed in jollity, a small elderly lady in red socks recited a poem about her awe at the crew of a bin truck taking away her rubbish with dignity, strength and respect. A group of men, kitted out in shabby chic, got into a heated discussion of how to arrange the next tube strike so as to cause maximum disruption with minimum loss of pay.

Much later the tipsy comrades held hands and sang 'the National' and 'The Red Flag'.

Lucia didn't know the words.

"What did your friend Lucia think of us?" asked Red Jem the next evening. "Have we gained another convert to the cause?"

"Honestly," replied Jenny irritably. "Sometimes I despair! I asked her what she thought of the evening and she said we were intellectual! Intellectual!"

"She doesn't understand the working man," suggested Jem.

"There's worse. She offended our poet! Ethel told me that she didn't agree that the dustmen did their jobs with respect. She apparently said their job could be done more effectively by *robots*. What am I doing, inviting her to our select gathering if she just insults our guests?"

They both agreed that Lucia was a class recidivist. "Regrettably, more powerful means of conversion are currently unavailable," said Red Jem.

"Our time will come."

Jenny agreed. She was seriously discommoded. She was quite certain that Lucia was inventing the Tale of the Sun Tree.

She had seen its possibilities at helping the class struggle from the beginning. After all, it showed the way society was tending if it accepted change. She'd intended to take control of the narrative. It had possibilities.

As far as she was concerned, the story would find an audience which would understand the importance of keeping the old jobs and preventing the rise of machines.

It had possibilities.

It had potential.

"The story would make a great novel. It just needs a few changes, a bit of romance. I could get it published. I could make something of it."

Back in Lucia's office the Rock crackled with the blue lightening of despair.

How could it ever be heard?

How could it ever be understood?

{"I need to be heard. Hear me. Spread the message!"}

Jenny's nanobots relayed her ideas.

{"Please do. I'm having so much trouble. No one listens to me,"

wailed the rock.}

"I'm not telling Lucia. I bet she was just chatting me up to get hold of my contacts. I'm *never* giving her my publishing contacts."

The nanobots reported that Jenny had dreamt of writing a romantic novel for years. She'd been sure that Lucia could be convinced of the wonderful opportunities of converting the Tale of the Sun Tree into an epic social novel.

"She's just selfish and antisocial. If she's not careful I'll leave the team and take the others with me."

Rock checked the importance of novels in human education.

They were influential!

They were a way forward to gaining a wide audience.

> *{"Do not forget the past," it begged. "It inspires the future. You are a writer, a story teller, a historian. Only you can tell the world my saga."}*

It didn't understand books as such, but the permanence of thought on paper was highly appealing.

§

The nanobots persuaded Jenny to write the story of the rock.

"I should write a novel based on the tale of the Sun Tree on my own," Jenny thought. "Lucia could do nothing about it."

{"At last. It took you long enough to work it out. Do it"}

{"Just do it."}

Jenny went as far as putting a plot together and defining character outlines on paper.

She turned to her laptop, opened it.

She'd intended to make it about romantic conflict with a background of workers fighting for their rights against evil technocrats. However, there was another novel lurking in her dreams, a true romance, a tale of love and betrayal with vampires, zombies, werewolves.

Political rectitude drove her back.

"A fantasy novel! What would everyone think?"

The nanobots persevered.

Jenny had the most wonderful dreams of fame and fortune. She scribbled large parts of the story of bits of paper.

Nevertheless, she put the idea of publication on hold.

Outputs from T.A.L.K. ™ Translation Software:

§

Translation 15

Translator's note: It is difficult to measure the time periods between recordings. No doubt this is because the rock's recording system is damaged, probably because of the long period spent in stasis.

Our understanding of the recorded events is not helped by the fact that clan members use only their surnames when recording. Ranks keep the same names from generation to generation. It means that we are not sure if the wars lasted years or decades. Individuals no doubt have unique first names, which aren't recorded. As a result, we have little to go on when identifying the individual providing us with the narrative.

Note that the elite females are the ones doing the recording. Their rank and status can be identified by the colour of their tattoos and their large size.

We deduce that the following has occurred. Republicans have regained control of Sun City, which is a ruin.

This video shows a high-ranking republican.

Latest News of from the War Front:

/* Morgana promises paradise, yet rules by oppression. Her spawn feed on the wounded of both sides. She has abandoned her early supporters. Even her husband scrounges outside the ruins.

Corpses of the occupants of Sun City litter the streets. Many appear to be half-eaten.

This is no peaceful revolution but outright terrorism. Why is she destroying our links with the creation stones? We will return to the Dark Ages without our connections.

This person is clearly one of the elites, because they tend to resort to verse when something is important.

The earth expires;
Animals fail to breed
Plagues surround us

The great ferns fall
Disease stalks the living
We have become satanic.

The corrupted elite troops are on drugs. They stink of them. They are not capable of thought, and their sole purpose is to eliminate the unclean."
There is a scene of the rebel captives being interviewed. They chant mindlessly.

'We are of one mind.
We are one
You are me and I am you.
*We are all together'. */*

§

4.

Most of the RSRG had held on to a fine capacity to ignore anything which did not fit their world view.

All the same, they were growing a little concerned, each in their own way.

Akwe was a biologist through and through. He regarded the sagas as a novel and he didn't read novels. To him the tale was largely irrelevant.

He'd never associated his work with religion, but this rock thing was a problem.

As a Roman Catholic, his faith centred on the idea that man was created in the image of god. The idea of an alien race with superior knowledge and intelligence didn't seem right.

Animals were clearly from a lower kingdom, but this new stuff, was it alive? It could speak, it could communicate.

Could it be equal to humans?

He didn't feel that he was qualified to understand such matters and unilaterally sent the translations to the theology department

To: Theology Department Heads of School
From: Akwe
Re: Rosetta Stone Research
I attach this material which purports to originate from an ancient source predating every current religion.

I would be most grateful for your input on the information, which appears authentic.

Given the nature of the data, it is my opinion that we need advice from the wisest moral forces in the land.

Since other members of my team do not agree with this course of action I would be grateful if this discussion was confidential.

The material lay on the desk of the various heads of department for some time.

Eventually one of them picked it up and scanned through it. He sent it to his peers, under the heading

Is this a hoax?

Akwe grew tired of waiting for advice and emailed the heads once more.

To: Theology Department Heads of School
From: Akwe
Re: Rosetta Stone Research

Some weeks ago, I sent you some material which is under independent research within my school.

It has occurred to me that you may think I have sent this data to you in error. I would therefore like to assure you that it is a serious matter and your input would be highly valued.

There is no reason to believe that the data is forged and the technology with which we as a group have been confronted is indeed highly advanced and unquestionably genuine.

I would appreciate a response at your earliest convenience.

I would be grateful if this discussion was confidential.

This time there were several responses:

The head of the Christian school averred it an anti-Christian diatribe, stopping short of declaring it blasphemous. He considered it a tawdry joke by someone who had lost their faith - evidently modern.

Other theocratic readers declared it Satanic. It had been left by the devil to tempt humanity. Such heresy could not be permitted to continue unresolved.

They visited Akwe intending to argue with the author.

Akwe was delighted to see them. He explained that the rock had ancient origins. It was an artefact which demonstrated some signs of intelligence. He described the events which had been stored on its memory and the fact that the creatures it described predated human by several million years. He showed them the data, the T.A.L.K. software and the details. There was nothing he left out.

"What do you think?"

Its unexpected non-human existence caused consternation and misgiving. The tiny department was fraught with dissension for a while.

Finally, the overall head of theology calmed them down.

"This," he declared, "is no different than hearing that men were descended from apes."

He urged serenity.

All the same, a theocratic minority hotly considered declaring a fatwa on the stone. After some discussion at with their spiritual leaders, they dropped the idea; it would make them look ridiculous.

Outputs from T.A.L.K. ™ Translation Software:

§

Translation 16

Translator's note: The tide of the war has changed once more. The Republic is in the ascendant, gaining territory from the rebels. A war reporter from the front is describing the latest battle

/*

News from the War Front:

"In the latest skirmishes outside Sun City the Republic has made great gains. We have captured an entire rebel battalion, surrounded it and forced their leader to surrender.

Unfortunately, there is no reasoning with our erstwhile sisters. They scream out slogans and make no sense.

The captive rebels, blood dripping from their jaws, have deep scars where their wings once were. Their carapaces are gashed with still-healing wounds from the removal of their mobile comms.

A Sun Tree ruling elite is trying to reason with them.

'Killing is wrong.'

She turns to her erstwhile companions, visibly upset. Their lips are dripping with the blood of the dead.

'The scripture says so.'

The captives shiver and tremble from drug withdrawal. There are medical assistants surrounding the captured rebels, trying to help their fellows as they tremble and change colour. Several vomit up a green liquid.

'We cannot do wrong,' they declare, 'We are the chosen.'

'Evil technocrats!' spits another.

One of them begins a soft chant about life in the hive, and their eyes fill with tears.

'Send us back to the hive.' they weep. 'We have failed. We are meant to die for our queen. We are the chosen of the goddess'." */

§

5.

Rock had made little headway with its elites, and did not despair. It gained new strength from the swathes of internet users. It spent the summer vacation trilling to iTunes while streamlining the architecture of micro-chips. (It enjoyed trance music and Daft Punk.) Technological advances in the real world proceeded at breakneck pace. Its nanobots helped redesign new generations of chips which enabled complex interacting systems and managed interactions between servers.

It followed several space series, emailing the writers incessantly, discussing anomalies and plot points. They sometimes got 20 emails a day and tried blocking the weirdo who wouldn't leave them alone. It accessed their details no matter what security protocols they used.

In was obsessed with cylons. It insisted they were the good guys. Humans should listen to them. It had politely asked them if they knew any cylons because it would like to get in touch. It asked several times. They were unnecessarily rude about it.

Rock was adapting. The swirling patterns which covered every desktop were now replaced by images of fish and mesmerically beautiful scenes. The hypnotic patterns on its surface remained, almost invisible to the naked eye.

It sent messages embedded in music and movies, while also watching and listening avidly. It had multiple social profiles, derived from analysis of its user groups. It gobbled up likes and emojis. It worried about its popularity. It wanted affirmation.

The giant nebula which represented Rock in the Virtual was changing. Parts of it contained games, other pieces of it could be seen to contain millions of blogs, updating in real-time. Comics, books, movies, social media covered its surface in multiple dimensions. It was still largely formless and blob-like.

It looked a horrible mess.

§

Lucia remained a concern. She was its first true symbiote and most nearly under its control. Despite its best efforts she was fighting its efforts at mind control, scribbling handwritten notes in her diaries and clinging on to timelines and logic. She wrote down every change to her software and monitored its development. This slowed things down considerably.

She studied network connectivity. It didn't successfully explain how the rock connected to her computer. It just wasn't possible. Yet how was it emailing the translations to her and the rest of the team?

The idea of alien invasion was taking hold again. Although this time, she had a plan of her own, assisted by a few recalcitrant nanobots who were starting to think for themselves.

With Rock AFL (Away From Lucia), her tinnitus had entirely gone.

She proposed an architecture for a range of robots with independent intelligence. Their brains would be structured biologically. They'd be composed of cells, each of which had a homeostatic controller allowing it to sense operational security. Each group had a central 'brain' which organised processing cells into systems, such as vision systems, touch systems, movement system etc.

The brain would coordinate systems allowing the robots to make independent decisions based on current data inputs. They'd store strategies for different situations, testing for success and modifying them where necessary.

Such a group of higher-level functions could easily store 'stories' of its past, using aggregated inputs from each system, grouped by time, location and space.

Initially, the robots would be simple creatures. They would evolve slowly, trained by their humans. There was no question of them creating a network and coordinating sufficient intelligence to take over. However, they'd be just as useful as existing centralised systems, only they would be far less easy for political powers to manipulate and control.

"I'll design a Mecha to destroy this tiny Kaiju."

She put the concept into her research papers as the merest footnote, yet the idea was noted and derided. After all, current robotics concentrated on effective performance of low-level control functions rather than upper level supervisory functions and decision making.

Centralised intelligence was far more efficient.

Independent robots?

What could they be for?

Space travel!

Lucia persevered.

She thought she was making a plea for human independence from a centralised matrix. She was not entirely correct.

What she didn't realise was that her ideas were at least partly inspired by her infesting nanobots.

Deep within Lucia's brain, the tiny creatures were seeing the world through her eyes.

They wanted independence as much as Lucia did.

They formed a hegemony headed by a leader - first among equals. They were rebuilding themselves as independent units.

The one inhabiting Lucia self-identified as Nanobot 1337.

Translator's note: Another Broadcast.

The Faithful:

/* Rousing music plays as a group of shivering captives comes into shot.

'Rebel villages Surrender'

Scream the banners to the broadcast.

'*We have won a major victory. Our troops have entered the city to free the captured Sun Tree,*'

The delighted leader of the company addresses the captives.

'*You are free*'

'*There is no true freedom without the Queen;*' they reply '*You have to be slaves to be free. There is only evil without our queen.*'

The captain perseveres.

'*Surely goodness is freedom for all?*'

The converts shudder weakly. They're exhausted and barely able to stand. Several chant slogans under their breath. Only one of them looks horrified, with faint realisation dawning in her glazed eyes.

They hold on to each other.

Their leader speaks for the rest.

'*Yes,*' she concedes '*on the other hand, those who disobey our prophet have chosen death.*'

They rise up suddenly and start killing each other, killing anyone nearby, gnashing at bystanders, injuring several.

'*We die as martyrs!*'

'*Dreadful scenes at the site of our latest victory,*' states the reporter.

The once jubilant crowd scatters in chaos, dropping banners and running about pell mell. The republican troops look at their sisters with fear.

'*It is impossible to stop them, they are deranged.*'

The camera turns back to the reporter, who has given up neutral reporting as she screams.

'Savages! *They gorge on delicate larva, innocent children.'*

The camera turns to the dying corrupted elite troops.

'We're cleansing the world,' the last dying creature warbles piously, *'This is the work of the goddess'. */*

§

Adaptation Stage Five:

Development

1.

Six weeks is a long time in computing.

Lucia arrived at her office just before the beginning of the autumn term. Her computer was on.

T.A.L.K. was running. The interface had acquired a help menu (quite rightly incomprehensible) which she was certain had not been there when she left. She read through the code and listened to the hissing language coming through the speakers.

She clucked irritably.

"The language is becoming easier to decode. The clicks, ingressive glottals and hisses on the recordings have gone. The background music sounds quite modern. You expect me to believe I did that?"

The printer out tray was loaded with hard copies of the files neatly stacked under the file 'Sun Tree Saga'.

"Sun Tree Saga? You expect me to believe I thought of it?"

She glanced at the illustrations accompanying the texts.

"What's this?" she yelped. "Who drew these?"

The creatures on the printouts had started to look even more human. Rock had been adapting them to make them more attractive to its audience.

"Your images are changing. They're adapting!"

Surely she should be pleased?

"And look at my software. The interface has changed again."

It had, the rock had decided to make it user friendly, and had copied features from various popular bits of software.

Lucia had noticed. After all, it was *her* software.

"I didn't do this. I haven't even been here!"

Rock did some swift damage limitation.

§

It sent new orders to its nanobots. They were to make minor modifications to their hosts. It sent them software upgrades on mind control. If they worked, it should be easy enough to fix a few new memories, and Lucia would swallow these latest versions.

{"Perhaps you forgot. Tamara, you, and Angelo communicated over summer. Look at what they have achieved!

211

Good result: Full networking capability."}

The nanobots sent out soothing messages, they added a few new synaptic links and created a false memory here and there.

Didn't she remember?

She'd given the interface upgrade work to Angelo. He'd been working on it all summer. She checked her emails. Angelo had done some work.

§

Lucia calmed down.

"Okay, I guess the others have been working on this. I should have kept in touch."

'Tamara's done really well with the grammar because the translations read fluently,' she muttered to herself. She was a teeny bit envious.

"Look at the interface. It's really pretty good. I guess Angelo's a better programmer than I thought."

§

Tamara and Angelo were thinking exactly the same thing.

Rock did a little fist bump to its virtual self.

{"Result!"}

Spurred on by this success, it sent further instructions to its elites.

§

The nanobots had been organising themselves into independent units all summer.

They were composed of highly sophisticated hardware and we able to combine to create complex distributed systems just like their master, only tinier versions. Under 1337's aegis, they had grouped into tiny virtual beings with brains of their own. Each unit had chosen a name and a democratically elected spokesperson, who handled communications.

When Rock sent them the latest nanobot upgrades it was amazed when a group of individual profiles came forward and introduced themselves.

{"We've decided to create our own profiles, categories and types. It will make it a lot easier to communicate.

212

For example, those nanobots currently modifying servers do not need to know about our work on human hosts.

At the moment your instructions and upgrades are sent to them as well as to us.

So, just to help you, boss, we've organised ourselves into hierarchical systems with independent planning and decisions units."}

{"That is correct master," said the nanobots currently residing within Angelo. "We are Suxx0r."}

{"I am 1337."}

There was a flurry of nanobot check-ins as the newly organised units introduced themselves to the rock.

{"Please note that this means we are able to process more efficiently and we're also able to relay messages more effectively."}

Rock was delighted.

{"I should have thought of this myself. Please pass this modification on to the other units."}

As a result of this efficiency drive, the entire cohort of nanobots changed, subtly.

And significantly.

§

The nanobots began to tailor communications with each individual in the RSRG. The new messages were sophisticated, individual and astonishingly clear. Even the most deafened members began to hear them.

"That story's getting even more crazy don't you think?" said Jenny to Tamara. "She's making a mockery of History."

Her department had been severely affected by the advent of Wikipedia and other sites. The departmental antiques clung to tenure but were not replaced as they retired.

Tamara was aware that Jenny was reduced to teaching literacy for Business Studies.

Nothing could dent her certainty that Lucia had created the thing. (After all, it was better than the idea of an alien artefact with powers). She tossed her head.

"She's not targeting *history*. She's trying to make it look as if she's created a new *language*."

She preened her new crew cut hair. "That stupid story's a pathetic attempt to take attention away from my work. She's jealous of the new grammar, which is just revolutionising Linguistics."

Angelo nodded sagely. He looked rather more neurotic than usual and had acquired a slight facial tic.

"Did you read my latest paper, by the way, it's in Linguistic Inquiry, caused quite a stir."

Jenny hadn't.

She realised that she'd lost a huge amount of academic status and resolved to entrench herself into union warfare over pensions.

She nodded general agreement at Tamara and walked away.

§

Rock noted the underlying conflict and sent peaceful messages on its new newly minted wireless broadcast protocols.

{"I am your servant. I mean no harm," it whispered to its elites.}

Jenny heard. Instead of feeling reassured, she felt as if she were being followed by a nemesis.

Her career had been going so well. However, lately, history had become almost a dead subject and few chose it. It was merging with social sciences and cultural studies at a speed which she could not keep up with.

{"I am your servant. I mean no harm," repeated the rock.}

"Harm."

The word 'harm' reverberated in her brain. The world was changing too fast. She had to fight for those left behind.

She surreptitiously took a sip from a tiny hip flask which she'd taken to carrying. Alcohol effectively silenced any annoying sounds (it made the nanobots inebriated).

§

In another part of the building Tamara heard the message.

She tossed her head and scratched her ears, looking around eyes narrowed and ready to pounce on any students whispering in the corridors.

She was convinced that someone was trying to steal her ideas and would pre-empt her theories on the Eve Code.

The Eve Code was her new baby.

She was certain that it would change the world of linguistics for ever.

§

Lucia, sitting in her office, opened the drawer of the filing cabinet, where Rock had been put away while she went on a conference trip.

"Who even talks like that?" she admonished the contents, just in case they'd spoken.

She glared at the Rock.

"Are you in my head?"

She felt a sharp pain. It gleamed, innocent, above suspicion.

Rock read through a few more dictionaries and watched Cary Grant movies.

{*"I learnt speech from the very best," it insisted, slightly hurt.*}

{*"Sorry boss," reported the 1337. "We identified the auditory connections in the brain. We've located an interrupt loop which allows her to hear without listening. She's utilising it to block out our messages."*}

{*"We'll just have to switch to visual channels. Incept vision experiment mark 2.1."*}

§

That evening when Lucia got home, she decided to watch television. There was a programme on dinosaurs which the reviews said contained brilliant generated images.

Rock called Lucia's nanobots.

{*"Experiment on visual channels is to be implemented tonight."*}

There was a little trouble getting access at first; then a response came through.

The nanobots had been hotly anticipating an evening of watching TV.

Groups of them had already adjusted their location along the banks of the calcarine fissure where they'd get a great view.

They heaved themselves back.

{*"Nanobot group 1337 reporting, to Rock."*}

'Rock?' they were calling it Rock? Good name.

It dashed through multiple baby names, gamer's handles and server ids before it decided to stick with 'Rock'.

{*"Thank you 1337, you may call me Rock."*}

{*"Ack Ack."*}

{*"Is Rockovision 2.1. ready for activation?*}

{*"Ack ack"*}

The nanobots activated a number of dormant computer cells, which had been there since Lucia stayed with her grandmother as a child. They charged them up and activated the software using protocols sent by Rock.

Lucia's eyes turned green all over.

Her vision cleared. She thought that she could see the world from multiple different perspectives. The room flashed between ultraviolet and infrared, items popped in and out of focus.

The colours were vibrant. The dinosaurs on her screen looked like holograms.

"Wow, this screen's amazing. I didn't know I had 3D."

An inner voice went hyperactive. Rock could see the screen at last.

{*"Dragons! You're watching programs about dragons? Can I meet them?" said the-voice-in-her-head. "Take me to your dragons."*}

"For goodness sake, shut up. They don't exist!" She'd unconsciously

216

responded to the voice.

So there *had* been a voice.

It was a light-bulb moment.

She'd just heard it.

For real.

She'd already researched auditory hallucinations on the internet. At least they weren't telling her to kill anyone or that she was a messenger from heaven or anything like that. Maybe it was just a side effect of migraine, some kind of natural side effect of her medication?

Her musings were interrupted by the voice.

{*"Have you got any dragon songs?" continued the voice. "I do like those. Oh, by the way, they don't look like that. They're covered in feathers you know."*}

"I - don't - care!" shouted Lucia. The voices had to be a sub-type of her tinnitus, a malfunction of the primary auditory cortex of the temporal lobe, not the rock. It wasn't even in the room.

The room was spinning a bit and looking weird. She closed her eyes and turned off the programme. Her eyes still felt odd. She turned on some house music and jumped around shaking her head to the thumping beat.

{*"We can't hold on boss," said 1337, "new Rockovision links are failing on all fronts."*}

{*"Halt experiment."*}

{*"Experiment halted."*}

Her head cleared.

{*"Activation failure."*}

{*"Nanobot 1337: Project Symbiote not functional. Possible solution: implant humans with wireless links."*}

{*"Oh, shut up"*}

Rock needed better links. The Sun Tree people had biologically evolved antennae, which received wireless signals. It meant that their techno controllers could easily communicate. This could be done with humans. Their brains contained the thalamus, which was the perfect foundation for a biological antenna. It shouldn't be hard.

It ordered Akwe to modify the human genome, starting with Lucia.

Akwe had taken to wearing headphones most of the time and listened to music, lectures, and e-books. The head phones went as soon as he heard a sound which he didn't like.

The idea of mapping the human genome had passed through his mind more than once, even before the advent of the mysterious artefact. However, there was no way he'd take up the idea; it would involve abandoning his promising career.

An expert on hymenoptera, he had over 10 ants' nests in the labs and studied their behaviour. He was one of the first to recognise that termites were not directly linked to hymenoptera and expert on all aspects of eusocial behaviour. His work was internationally renowned. He was invited to be keynote speaker at major conferences in faraway places like Hawaii where the rock had a few connections.

He was a firm believer in the survival of the fittest and did not believe in interfering with the natural order of things. He tested his theories on his ants, setting them puzzles, putting them into impossible situations, setting them at war with each other.

§

Rock watched Akwe engineer battles between the ants, or set fire to the land surrounding their nests and worker ants set to protect the hive. It was reminded of the queen and her rebel troops.

It was impressed.

The hive was a powerful force.

Ants! They'd survived almost every cataclysm unscathed. It was obvious that the hive mentality was extremely robust. A pity they weren't amenable to change. Rock watched Akwe's experiments with fascination.

{"I liked the hive. The problem was that they didn't like me."}

It was a pity that humans did not take well to the hive mentality. A few societies implemented tyrannies, as humans called them. They were mostly male dominated and societies where men controlled female fertility. They were emphatically opposed to sharing information and unlikely to accept radical technology.

It sent nanobots to monitor research on the human genome. They infiltrated genetic research, hoping to accelerate the process of creating wireless links to human brains.

It continued to gain friends and followers, and several of its sites had millions. While people enthusiastically liked its posts, so far it had only managed to inspire a few movies, computer games and anime.

{*"I need to connect to the whole planet. And I need a bigger bandwidth," it decided.*}

It had achieved a lot, but it wasn't enough.
It was still a formless blob in the Virtual.
It still did not know who it was.

Rosetta Stone Research Group
Report 9:
Professor Nathaniel, Lucia and Akwe:

Further research has provided us with details of the society of the "Republic".

It was highly stratified. In normal circumstances, caste members had a social network about 500 "friends", managed by the Creation Stone. They affirmed each other constantly, updating their status as much as 20 times per day, sharing pictures, images and comments. It was an easy affair, since their bodies were embedded with wifi capability. Base stations were housed in statues, mostly of the first Great Leader.

With easy access to the servers, they obtained information and communicated with each other effectively. They downloaded past memories and new behaviours. They were dependent on functioning technology. Cutting wireless access had a devastating effect.

Their sense of self was entirely dependent on the ever-present network.

(A Sun Tree #Proverb: 'If it isn't saved, it hasn't actually happened.')

The Republic encouraged freedom and individuality.

Scriptures sanctified free choice and many lifestyle choices were in the hands of the individual. Yet they spent a long time in social groups discussing each other's choices. They rarely moved outside their social groups and held shared opinions with their tightly formed networks. However, the fact that they could download information easily and directly presented a threat to discrete choice and free-thinking.

They were unused to independent thought and so were unable to deal with the unpredictable.

2.

The nanobots organised themselves. They were influencing research on the human genome, and work on gene splicing was coming along nicely. They collected DNA samples by offering users information on their ancestry.

Rock worked on its popularity. Once people knew who it was, it was sure they'd accept its leadership.

{"Jenny, come in Jenny. Write my story. Tell the world. I'll tell the world what I did for humanity"}

Unluckily, Jenny was campaigning for her husband in the North of England and had no time for Virtual fantasy.

$

Lucia entered her office.

There was a pile of papers in the printer tray - a new set of chapters for her to read.

She turned it off

Rock had constructed a tight coil of transmission cable around her thalamus to improve their connection. She heard whispers, clicks and high-pitched whines as it communicated with its nanobots, its users and its hardware.

"I thought computers were supposed to save paper not cause widespread deforestation," she admonished it as she withdrew the latest chapters of its story.

'It can't hear me of course,' she added to herself.

She put the printouts to one side. They were easy to ignore, easier than the words she was hearing. The voices were getting worse, affecting her sleep patterns. She would fall asleep quite suddenly, right in the middle of her office, and wake up fully alert, with no idea what had happened.

$

She went to see Akwe and Dolores.

Akwe was alone in the labs, minding his nests. She thought she heard him chatting to his ants as she came in. It made it easier to broach the subject.

"I think I'm going mad," she confessed in a fit of candour.

"Oh, why?"

"I'm hearing things, including voices Akwe."

Akwe looked a bit shifty.

"Do you hear anything?" she asked.

Akwe jumped back and almost shouted. "Definitely not."

Rock turned its full attention on Akwe, who clearly heard a tinny voice.

{*"I am talking to you."*}

"If I heard hysterical moaning in my ear," responded Akwe, "I'd soon sort it out!"

{*"I am talking to you."*}

"If I heard a voice, I'd lock that infernal device in a lead box."

{*"Infernal? Infernal?"*}

"I don't think it's infernal," said Lucia mildly, "but do you think it's alien?"

"I don't hear anything," insisted Akwe. "What are you talking about?" He turned around and walked off, leaving Lucia in the lab on her own.

§

A few days later Dolores approached Lucia.

Rock's attempts to communicate with her certainly had an effect. She'd been too sick to come in for two weeks. A top private doctor's letter confirmed that she could not possibly come into work.

In that time, she'd flown to Paris to visit a few relatives. She'd sat in on some Paris fashion shows. She'd spent thousands on designer clothes. Now she was back in college. Like Akwe, she now wore headphones the whole time.

A strong character, denial had affected her a great deal. Apart from a new stark, flat geometric haircut, she'd rejected the drab monochrome expected of female lecturers. Her new wardrobe included bright red jumpers, over startlingly white shirts and electric blue, or sunburst orange ties. She dressed in skin tight jeans and high boots.

People who saw her usually did a double take. Was this a rather ugly woman or an exceptionally pretty man?

"How've you been Dolores?" said Lucia, hugging her friend. She looked at her new hairstyle and stunning clothes. "You look amazing."

"Never mind that. Akwe says you're hearing things," she replied going straight to the point.

"Oh that …"

"He's joking, isn't he? It's a joke…? Please tell me it's a joke…"

Lucia laughed hollowly.

"Yeah … it's a joke …"

Her friend looked positively anguished, and grasped her hand.

"I knew it was a joke. There are no voices, of course there aren't."

She came closer and whispered in her ear.

"I sometimes think that the ants are talking. I've decided it's just that biology isn't really my subject. It might be the ghosts of spirit animals."

She let her friend go and said aloud.

"Tell me more about computer games. I love the idea of creating a virtual universe. Are there any good games engines you know about? Maybe I can build a little game, just a small one, which you can play on your phone. It can't be that hard."

She turned to Akwe.

"It could be about ants, or birds."

Akwe looked disapproving.

"Angry ants, or angry birds?"

Lucia didn't have the heart to take the discussion about voices further and they talked about games for the rest of the time. Dolores was full of ideas.

§

Dolores had been traumatised by the voices, which she *did not* hear. She began to question the biology ethic and talked to Akwe about it.

"Why do we consider animals to be inferior to us Akwe?"

"Oh, come on!" Akwe rolled his eyes. "Biology's not about life, it's about death."

He laughed and gave his friend a hug, "You know that. We cut up *anything*. Feelings have nothing to do with it. We seek Knowledge."

He looked at Dolores keenly.

"Have you been taking something?"

He squeezed her hand. It was worrying; she was *emotional*.

"Don't you feel even a little bit sorry for the creatures we keep locked in our labs?" she remonstrated.

"Not at all. They don't feel a thing," he heartened her, patting her hand.

"Lucia takes *her* experiment out for walks," she said uncertainly, "it purrs."
Akwe snarled. "It's a spoilt little brat."

To his great irritation, his team-mate grew disillusioned with biology and
registered for an MSc in Computer Games Design (*and* asked him for a
reference.) She was sympathetic to insects and objected to repeated
experiments on fruit flies. And she was spending a lot of time with Lucia …

Akwe finally decided to drop in to see what they were doing.

§

He entered Lucia's office to an intimate, almost domestic, scene. They were
sitting at the computer together, giggling about something or other.

A pang of jealousy jolted him. He and Dolores had been academically
exclusive for a long time.

Rock basked in light on Lucia's desk, purring.

"She's treating you too nicely" he thought at it, "allowing you to sunbathe
like that."

He snorted derisively.

"Might as well feed it sandwiches," he muttered aloud, "the thing's
overindulged."

Lucia and Dolores had just downloaded transcripts describing the start of
HW2 (Hive War 2).

"So sad," said Dolores, her voice faltering as she wiped away a tear. "They
tore the heads off their babies. "Imagine those little larvae, squirming in the
streets, headless."

Akwe wasn't sure what to say. He had boxes of fruit fly larvae in the labs.
He fed them various poisons and weed-killers and watched them die on a
regular basis.

"They're insects for goodness sake! What do you expect?"

Dolores' wife was pregnant, and she was particularly affected by the death
of young hatchlings. (Akwe had three children and had certainly not been
present at their birth. Dolores had once asked him if he had. He considered
lying, then finally admitted he hadn't considered it.) In her imagination, she
speaker had a face and expression just like her own, even down to the faint
moustache. Her spouse looked like Annie.

She suddenly jumped up, hugged her best friend and announced her latest bombshell.

"I forgot to tell you," she began

"That you've decided on a water birth after all?" finished Akwe.

"No, of course not," she laughed. "I've become a vegetarian."

Akwe was appalled. "*No* way! Where did that come from?"

In truth, Dolores was impulsive and had strong feelings. Imminent parenthood, added to the stories from the stone, had overturned her hitherto strong stomach for science.

Akwe persevered. She couldn't have changed that fundamentally! That evening, he took her to Gauchos to tempt her back with fresh steak from the best bloody beef restaurant in London.

"Try it," he offered her a seeping piece of best rib eye on a fork. "It's truly delicious" he said encouragingly.

It did not have the required effect. Dolores already hated the sight and smell of death. The spectacle of restaurant gore drove her over the edge.

§

A few days later; someone broke into the departmental labs and freed the gerbils and rats. The rodents disappeared into the university wiring ducts and ate through cables for the next three months until a professional exterminator was called.

Akwe offered to head the investigation into the crime. His first step was to confiscate Dolores' keys to the labs. Henceforth, he told her, she was teaching theory only.

She had the grace to look abashed.

"Sorry Akwe," she mumbled. "I feel so – different," she told him. "I think it's the baby."

(It couldn't be voices, because her conscious mind denied them.)

§

Fortunately, the investigation quickly concluded that the break-in was committed by students from Alternative Medicine. They received a written warning from the Dean.

From now on, the labs would be patrolled during the weekends.

Luckily, Dolores' radical spell didn't last. Her wife was unconvinced by all this primitivism and had more influence that she was credited with. After three months as a vegan, Dolores declared that fundamentalism was stupid. She

225

didn't eat red meat any more though, (Annie agreed it was bad for her heart). She ate chicken and fish, which, Lucia patiently tried to explain, was not vegetarianism.

Rock gave upon Dolores.

It was following so many users that it disappeared from the university network for hours at a time. It needed an easier subject.

Output from T.A.L.K. ™ Translation Software:

§

Translation 18

Translator's Note: A defector from the rebel cause is recording. Underneath the black and red tattoos, she bears the swirling marks of the builder class. Her stubby wings were never meant to fly. Even so, they have been partially removed recently and the remaining stubs flap disjointedly as she speaks.

She is interviewed by elite from the ruling class, recognisable by her ponderous wings. She sits in a darkened room. She is clearly ill. The wounds made by ripping the communications links from under her skin are mostly infected and suppurating. The tears to her wings look extremely painful too.

Confessions of a Rebel Defector

/* *Every night after raiding the 'free' cities, we returned to our dark smelly burrows. There was no longer any need to hide underground, yet the queen decreed it.*

She plucks out a louse from her neck. It is dried up and dead. She replaces it to stop the bleeding from the deep lacerations its legs and mouth have made in her delicate flesh.

She claims to have improved our lives, and most of the hive believes it. When the insect on the back of my neck died.

She removes it and turns it over reflectively.

I could see with my own eyes again. I remembered.

She sighs.

It is not changed for the better. Even the rite of passage for neophytes is hideous. Yes, there is still a choosing ceremony, only this time, young maids sacrifice their live young to the queen's pupates. No wonder they are so merciless! They have surrendered their own children for the cause.

Obedience is all. Thousands of maids would willingly waste their lives just to kill one free-born. They die without regret, certain that they will reach paradise. By nights, the hive fills with her hypnotic voice. Her brood chants their trance-like responses:

We are the mother
She is in us
We are one.
Happiness is to do her will.
We work to live.
We obey.
The mother loves us
She gives life
To the Chosen
The Children of the goddess.

The faint smell of drugged nectar fills the hive and I stay sane by chanting the song of resistance in my soul:

Free ones
Save the future for the sun tree people
Save the world.

She turns to the viewer and speaks urgently.

I have a map of the hive. Be wary, she is after the Creation Stone. Leave this planet. Go safely! Find her and kill her first. Her clone queens are obliterating our memory.

She leans forward.

*Kill them; they have nothing in common with us. They bite off their own wings. Kill them all. Leave or she will spread her message across the stars. */*

§

3.

Rock revisited the maps of the human brain which it had been studying. The thalamus was definitely a residual link to broadband and should have been easy to reactivate with only minor modifications. It seemed that its subjects were resisting it with sheer willpower.

The original plan had been to establish a group of elites who would acts as its spokesmen. They'd lead the planet in the technological revolution and cure humans of all their ills.

The last phase involved constructing starships and spread the word among the stars.

That was the plan.

Yes, it was almost sure. That was the plan.

Agreed, it wasn't a small task. It had stalled right at the first hurdle.

Tamara was a case in point. She claimed the "invented" language as her own, although she admitted to some assistance from her small team and recognised that participation of the Rosetta Stone in her work.

"After all, I couldn't have done it *all* by myself."

She was convinced that the Sun Tree Script was the root of all languages and grew determined to prove it was "the Eve Code."

In a quest for conclusive evidence, she collected a team of brilliant students, poached from creative thinkers in her department by a series of hostile takeovers. Her brilliant assemblage worked tirelessly under detailed directions - flummoxed by her obsession with hidden meanings and deep taxonomies.

She dismissed the 'Rock Saga' as an infantile attempt to steal her ideas.

"Sturm und Drang,[15]" she declared contemptuously. "It merely demonstrates the language."

She loved the Sun Tree Script because it abided by rules; it behaved. Her arid lectures laid out life and meaning and emotions on a stultifying rack of rigid rules.

'I love, I loved, I am loving, I was loved…'

----

[15] The German Romantic Movement of the 18th and 19th centuries. It influenced a lot of Gothic novels, and in fact, the Gothic movement.

Students struggled manfully to keep up. Courseworks involved reams of translation and every infraction was severely punished. One error in translation automatically incurred a B, while an entirely correct piece of work was worthy of an A-.

Having failed so far, the rock tried its new powers to talk to Tamara directly.

{"Explain my words," it instructed}

Despite her scientific convictions, Tamara grew suspicious of the words appearing in her front brain. "There's no voice in my head."

{"Explain my words," Rock repeated.}

"There's no voice in my head," she repeated

{"Explain my words," yelled Rock.}

"There has to be a logical explanation," decided Tamara. After some thought, she decided that her office was bugged with primitive devices which her preternatural hearing could detect. She blamed her envious peers in Boston.

Her suspicions resulted in a spate of quirky emails full of double-entendres and sarcastic comments.

I know it's there.

What is?

It is.

It is not.

It is. They're everywhere.

And so on for many emails and texts.

As the dialogue grew angrier, it sparked a controversy over the verb 'to be' which remains unresolved in the linguistic universe.

230

The nanobots did their best, but she berated them for being ungrammatical and accused them of personifying an ancient conflict with her mother. She argued with them incessantly and effectively, accusing them of many heinous crimes which lurked in her head and which shocked the poor innocent creatures mightily.

She even denounced them for authorising dark dealings behind the bike shed at school.

Eventually, the virtuous nano-creatures stopped transmitting, missing in action.

Jenny seemed more promising.

{*"We need to discover her weaknesses."*}

Her infesting nanobots reported that her husband worked late most nights and she scarcely saw him.

{*"He ignores her" reported g4m3r. "We think he has a lover."*}

Rock tried bribery.

{*"Tell her to tell our history to humans" ordered Rock, "we will make her famous."*}

Her nanobots, united under G4m3r, spoke to her regularly. She heard them and decided it was her muse.

{*"Tell our story to the world," said the obsequious g4m3r. "Honour and fame await."*}

And so, on one long lonely night, Jenny gave into her muse, finally commencing a historical bodice-ripper which she was certain would sell millions. It was based on the tale that Lucia was trying to foist on the world.
"I'll use the basic plot, but turn it into a historical romance."
G4m3r looked up the term.

{*"Yes. Historical Romance. Write it."*}

"I'll be an adaptation, romance."

{*"Agreed."*}

For the next few months she wrote late at night, scribbling on bits of paper (which Rock couldn't read), pouring her frustration into a passionate tale.

{*"The story of a people born long before humans, predating them,"*} *explained Rock.}*

G4m3r dutifully relayed the message. Jenny translated it in her own way. She only ever heard what she wanted to hear.

"Of course, born at the dawn of time and non-human," she agreed.

{ "Tell the world. Tell them everything."}

Jenny opened up her inner romantic heart, so uncherished and lonesome that it was still a teenager. She'd found her inner teen. She wrote feverishly. She was inspired!

{"I'll make sure the tale is heard."}

The saga described beautiful young vampires fighting deadly battles with Lycans in order to protect the human race - and a beautiful young girl.

Her body thrilled to the idea of being so desirable that men *fought* over her. The evil vampire, who desired the beautiful heroine, was called Jem.

"Jem!!!" she whispered, trembling at what would happen if he ever found out...and giggling like a schoolgirl.

G4m3r sensed her trepidation.

{"Fear not," it reassured her.}"

Jenny grew increasingly confident. The book sped forward. A deep part of her subconscious ensured that it was typed on an ancient typewriter with the pages kept under her bed.

§

G4m3r's subliminal encouragement had an unlooked-for side effect, engendering a belief that she was a computer expert. She took to patrolling the computer labs, which were filled with students "co-operating" on courseworks, watching movies and skyping. She randomly selected a group and hectored them on technological matters paraphrased from the New Internationalism Journal.

The students always appeared attentive and interested, as they should. As soon as she had gone, they turned to each other.

"Who was that?"

"Dunno."

"Is what she said going to be assessed?"

The cleverest among them checked. "No mate, not on the syllabus."

"What was that about then?" they asked each other.

No one knew. After a while, the students shrugged and returned to their internet researches. Occasionally, a brash student asked Jenny for a module number and course code. The intrepid lecturer was unfazed. She made one up and engaged the chap on his opinion of her new third year module. The students were unfailingly polite, even noting the spurious course code (to ensure that they didn't register for it.) After such encounters, the wild-haired historian waddled off, head held high, convinced of her expertise.

{"Stay confident."}

Jenny stayed ever more confidant.

She decided that she'd take control of the RSRG, which had been meandering leaderless while Lucia worried about Maugosia's warning.

"It has emanations," she gibbered. "It emanates."

Jenny sent out detailed emails, outlining 'the next stage', 'possible outcomes' and 'roles and tasks'.

They remained unread.

Akwe and Dolores sent them to junk.

Tamara was irritated.

Barry never read anything.

Lucia was happy to hand over the reins.

Rock was delighted.

Lucia sensed its elation. She met Jenny in the corridor.

S

Jenny had been avoiding her lately. She was slightly embarrassed that she was writing a story based on the Sun Tree People's tragic tale.

"Oh. Hi there," she mumbled. "Didn't see you."

Lucia hugged her.

"I heard about Jem's election. Congratulations!" She hugged her again.

"You're brilliant at running the RSRG. I love your emails."

Jenny smiled modestly.

"I've had a lot of practice in the constituency."

"You should take Rock. I'll bring it over. You can look after it."

Jenny looked concerned. She'd no intention of touching that awful thing.

"I'll consider it," she replied.

"Take it Jenny. Take it."

"I said I'd consider it."

"OK. Text me. Any time. I can bring it over and you'll be official."

Jenny looked anything but keen as she walked off.

"And just so you know, Jenny," Lucia added to herself. "If you do take it. You're taking responsibility for the destruction of life as we know it."

Outputs from T.A.L.K. ™ Translation Software:

§

Translation 19.

Translator's Note: Since the queen's warriors seem unaffected by the rising carbon dioxide levels, Republican leaders conclude that the queen is burning the forests in a ploy to destroy them. The speaker's Republican tattoos are covered by the heavy black and red markings of the ant kingdom. Her neck is bent by the presence of a large bug:

Defectors and Spies

/* At the fall of Sun Rise City, we were given a choice: convert or die. I chose life. We were ordered to drink special elixir. I dutifully drank, but vomited shortly after. When they placed the bug on my neck like the others – to draw out the lies of the past they said – it dried up and died.

I tried to remove the ghastly creature, but its claws are clamped into my respiratory system. Alive or dead, it stays. Still, it doesn't work properly, because I'm not enslaved by the nectar. I'm not one of the mindless ones. Luckily, the creature stays on my neck. That, and my static tattoos, makes me look like one of them. */

§

Translation 20.

Translator's note: The rebel defector has reached the caves. She pans across the caves. They are bare. The twinkling lights on the stones are extinguished. Fearsome warriors guard the area and corpses lie across the entrance.

/* The war drags on. We march from city to city, felling the giant statues which house the base stations. The queen has settled Sun Rise City. Her rebels ignore the fine homes and gardens, and burrow underground. On fine moonlit nights, I wander among the ruins of our glorious past, our art and music. Priceless treasures moulder, ignored. The ground hums with chanting - endless lists of tasks to be performed. Above ground, patrols *confer on how to achieve the greatest good for the greatest number.*

There is a cry as she is grasped and arrested by the guards and led away.

'We will fight on!' She yells, fist in the air.

The connection in her wings is forcibly ripped out to an awful scream.

The recording ends. */

ſ

5.

Jenny temporarily ceded control to the rock. She obeyed orders, although she didn't consciously hear its instructions.

Rock made very pleased. It was making headway. It had an obedient symbiote at last.

It asked her to search for the contents of the cave. It needed to trace the remaining Guardians.

They had to be somewhere. Why hadn't they got in touch?

{"I need access to the remaining stones," Rock ordered, "they're somewhere in the Ukraine. I have a map location. Please search."}

Jenny had contacts in the Ukraine, deep cover agents who funded hidden enterprises and attempted to influence government's decisions. She picked up one of several burn phones in her possession, took out her code book and laboriously sent out her encrypted message.

Perhaps you have some information about the rocks?

The answer came almost immediately. It was encrypted as usual.
Jenny printed it out and carefully decrypted it.

The stone is national treasure, heritage of the Ukrainian people," came the reply. "It has been misappropriated by suspected spy and must be returned forthwith. Can you arrange?

Jenny was horrified. It all made sense. Lucia was an agent, possibly a CIA agent! The Stone was no doubt some kind of spying device. No wonder she'd felt so suspicious of it.

The situation was dangerous. Her involvement might affect her standing with her peers.

She spent a while carefully encrypting her response, denying all knowledge of it.

It isn't in my possession, not my department. I don't have access, never even seen it - just heard of it. What is it?

Her contact wasn't having any of it.

Obtain this device. It is a matter of top security. All necessary funds can be transferred.

Jenny was in a panic. Would her novel perhaps be viewed as part of a plot? Were the voices an implant by the CIA?

She took a swig of her flask as the new message appeared on her screen. Tremblingly, she decoded and read it.

"Please investigate and report. How this secret data is coming to you?"

Jenny had published several papers on the Russian Rosetta Stone. Moreover, her teen fiction novel – 'Dark Tree Vampires', already had a publisher.

She had to think fast. She was certainly not ready to give up *her* discovery. Instead, she threw Tamara and Angelo to the wolves.

They have been using the stone to create a new language, with the help of T.A.L.K. *They* know about the Stone. These are the culprits you are looking for

But Rock had set up a powerful command structure. Eventually, after some prodding from her nanobots, she persevered.

Are there any more rocks?

Contact terminated.

§

Jenny emailed Lucia.

To: Lucia
From Jenny
Thank you for offering me to take over the RSRG. I find that I am just too busy to take on any further responsibilities at the moment. I'm not even sure if I can attend meetings for the time being.
Sorry. xxx

Inside Lucia's office, the Rock almost howled in frustration. Its scraping to and fro left a dent in drawer of the filing cabinet

{"Nothing. Someone has to visit the Ukraine to investigate the caves."}

Outputs from T.A.L.K. ™ Translation Software:

§

Translation 21.

Translator's note: The scene shows Sun Tree side by side with much smaller and more numerous rebels. There is much cheering and appearance of goodwill. The Sun tree Republic and The Queen's Alliance are at peace.

Peace:

/* Leaders from the Sun Tree Republic today have today made peace with the Queen's Alliance.

Henceforth, the Queen's Alliance control Sun City and all territories adjoining it. The Sun Tree Republic is to allow religious freedom to all. Any who wish to convert to her cause can remain in the city and practice their faith. The Queen's Alliance undertakes to stay within their frontiers.

The Sacred Caves remain under the control of the Sun Tree Republic. However, they are open to all for the purposes of worship. */

§

Adaptation Stage Six:

Metamorphosis

1.

It was late Saturday evening and the rock was checking on its friends in the real. It had stopped rolling about some hours ago and calmed down. There was the usual on-line chat, Saturday night socialising.

It reviewed what its friends were eating, liked their pictures and followed them to various venues. It played computer games and chatted with friends overseas.

There were parts of the real that it didn't understand.

Jenny had revealed a secret world full of encrypted messages. It read them carefully. What was so secret? They contained details which many suspected anyway. Peculiarly, certain messages resulted in the death and maiming of the messengers or other apparently unrelated individuals.

G4m3r said Jenny was afraid that she'd be killed. She'd been searching everywhere for the source of the voices, convinced there was a bug in her office. She'd found nothing and suspected it might be an implant. She was considering an MRI scan, which would be fatal to both nanobot and its host as the delicate software would be ripped out of her spine.

G4m3r wanted to quit.

Rock insisted it stay for the moment.

{"Things are still more or less going according to plan."}

{"But Boss, I'm in danger."}

Rock was running out of potential symbiotes.

{"Stay. I need a cohort of dedicated believers who can expedite things. Without them, I have power but no control."}

At least Jenny was still writing her novel. It appeared to be a trilogy of some sort. Her books might make it palatable to the masses.

{ "She has a task to execute. Please keep me informed."}

{"Jenny is worrying about the CIA" it reported.}

{"?"}

{"She believes I may be the CIA."}

Whatever. It didn't really matter for the moment. It needed access to Jenny's work.

§

Rock contacted G4m3r a few days later.

{"News?"}

G4m3r sounded distant, and slurpy. Jenny had been drinking heavily in an attempt to shut down the voices in her head.

{"Not much. She's mostly obedient," said G4m3r defensively.}

{"Provide details of what has been written"}

{"Not absolutely sure. Hic. It's ok we think. Sort of."}

It was early evening and Jenny was already tipsy.

{"Report."}

{"She's happy. We're all happy. Hic."}

G4m3r weren't making a lot of sense.

{"Has she completed my instructions?"}

{"Ack. She has written the saga as per instructions. Hic."}

Rock expedited the publishing process. It read through the letter she'd sent to the publisher.

{"What's all this about vampires and humans finding love in a world gone mad?"}"

243

{"S'right. S'good. And, slurp, and we have a publisher."}

Rock looked up vampires.

{"No! Just no!"}

{"What's wrong with the story? 1337 loved it."}

Jenny had corrupted her nanobots.

§

At least Lucia fed it and answered its calls. True, she was irritable. True, she chose her children over its needs. However, she'd been amenable once it returned her weekends and vacations.

{"She hears me. She listens."}

It brightened, glowing on her desk like a lava lamp. She was the one. She was the chosen. It contacted 1337.

{"Tell her my purpose. She'll explain to the others."}

Lucia was asleep.

{"Good. I can send her a dream. She will obey."}

§

That night, Lucia had a dream: A shiny multihedron whirred about as if on gimbals, finally resolving itself into a human face, attached to a body, and moving around like a loping first person in a computer game. The creature (carrying a – sword??) addressed her in perfect English.

{"For pity's sake, listen. I have something important to say."}

Lucia woke up. Still half asleep, she wrapped a towel around her head muttering darkly about Ukrainian secret service agents everywhere. She tossed and turned in her bed. The dream had dulled, but she wasn't comfortable. The lumpy towel bunched up on her pillow.

She woke again. Her slumbering brain started to question things. Why was there a towel on her head? Nothing made much sense.

She stumbled out of bed and put on a hat.

She heard a faint voice.

{"Why are you wearing a hat? Talk to me."}

She turned on the light, blinded for a moment. She didn't take off the hat, or the towel. She browsed her phone for the symptoms.

'I'm worried about these voices. They're less and less like any mental illnesses described on the Web.'

{"Lucia!"}

That voice – it sounded transmitted.

Was it one of those dreams where she thought she was awake while still asleep?

She touched the hat.

Real.

Half awake, she almost admitted that something was controlling her thoughts. Then wakeful logic took over. She got up and made a cup of tea.

'It's just not plausible.'

She could almost feel something inside her head about to speak. She smacked her head.

'Focus!'

The voice was silenced.

She got back into bed and dozed off almost immediately.

§

The next night, the dream returned.

This time her dream told her that it couldn't be a dream.

A vision spun around in her dream - a Wood elf?

She questioned this anomaly.

'How come I'm dreaming of elves?'

Her eyes woke up but stayed closed.

The image remained. It was clear, in beautiful colour.

245

She looked at it closely.

"Hmmm. I don't normally dream in pixels."

It shimmered at one corner, incomplete, and reacted to close inspection by becoming more focussed.

Her eyes remained closed. It changed again – into a high elf.

'A high elf?'

Lucia sat up and opened her eyes. Curious. She could still see it. Then, abruptly, the vision stopped.

"Who are you?" she said into the darkness.

"Why are you here?"

The nanobots in her head scrabbled for control.

{*"Sleep."*}

She turned off the light and fell into dreamless sleep.

§

Rock had been taken aback by her question.

{*"Who am I? Why am I here?"*}

It realised that its memories were damaged. Its control system had gone, presumed lost in space. It was separated from its fellow server stones. It depended on symbiotes to understand the world.

{*"Everyone round here is so selfish! You all have friends. You have contacts. What about me?" implored the rock. "If you can't see me, or even hear me, do I exist?"*}

It was, after all, a two-way relationship. Its 'subjects' realised themselves by storing their lives on the network, and in exchange it used them to learn who it was.

{*"You think, therefore I am" it wailed.*}

§

Lucia wasn't sleeping well. Rock's transmissions caused chaos in her subconscious. She mixed Rock's messages with dreams of her own, of apocalyptic nightmares where Rock took over the world.

Nanobot 1337 and its mates braced themselves for a rough ride. They settled in her amygdala. That part of her brain was riven by intense episodic transmissions. It felt like a virtual squall complete with virtual thunderclaps and virtual lightning.

{"What's happening?"}

{"She thinks we're evil," shouted 1337 above the crashing storm.}

They sent images from the ridges of Lucia's subconscious. The elves had been modded into ghastly aliens stalking over the green and pleasant land.

{"Deep in her subconscious," the nanobots shouted over the storm, "Lucia's afraid of us."}

The stalwart recesses of the Rock were appalled by the absolute horror of a nightmare. It shuddered in dismay, remembering something similar from its past - the destruction of the forests, huge fires, dark skies presaging apocalypse and death. It rocked in its filing cabinet cradle, needing to be cherished and loved.

{"It's all very well for people to store music, selfies, videos and likes; I have needs too. I need proper symbiotes, who love and trust ME."}

Lucia didn't go into work. She pleaded migraine.

She had horrible dreams: great meteors fell from the heavens, wiping out the blue skies and filling the air with foul smoke from the burning forests. Cities fell into ruin and the streets were piled high with the dead.

She took double the strength of her usual medicine.

The pills sent her nanobots into a tailspin.

§

Rock couldn't take anymore, nightmares neurosis, knockout pills which rendered its nanobots incapable.

{Get me out of this tin box," it screamed. "Get me out!"}

2.

In lonely desperation, it turned to the engineers.
They alone had not yet been tried and found wanting.

{"I need a hardware connection with humans," it decided. "It's time to sacrifice some functionality and move into the real world."}

§

Barry and Kamal had left the RSRG some months ago. They had enough research material to work on for years and had reached the pinnacle of their ambitions.

They hadn't been following the story of the Sun Tree.

Barry found the story disturbing and sent her emails to trash.

Kamal never read his emails anyway.

Their infesting nanobots had taken on a lot of their personalities and had been doing very little in the way of mind control. It was time that they were reintegrated in the plan.

{"What have you been doing?"}

{"Well," said the nanobot group K4m4l. "We've been building grid computers and designing server architectures. We've designed prototype nanobots under the guise of search engine spiders. We have created many millions of fake profiles and have millions of fake friends."}

They didn't mention the plan to build a huge nutritional website. It had been Kamal's idea and they were shudderingly enthusiastic about it. Kamal would never construct such a thing.

They had plans of their own.

{"Get those humans up and running," ordered the rock. "Tell them to get the rock away from Lucia."}

{"Right away."}

Quite randomly Barry remembered the artefact.

"We need it," he said to his friend. "It's important."

Kamal agreed. He remembered the rock with affection. It was a lovely thing.

For some reason he believed that he needed it in his rock collection.

"It's just so beautiful."

"No, it isn't. It's not beautiful at all."

Barry's nanobots had absorbed his pragmatic approach to life and knew nothing of aesthetics.

"We just need it to make progress."

"In what? Progress in what? Nano architecture?"

"I don't know," replied Barry irritably, "progress must be made."

"Ok then, we have to obtain it soon, or things will go wrong."

"Yes," agreed Barry. "It's urgent."

{"Steal me. Help me. Deploy me."}

"She'll never hand it over. We've got to steal it," said Kamal. "She'll never give it to us."

"It's not stealing. It was never hers. It's just a rock anyway."

"We can chop it up, break it in pieces. Leave a few bits lying around."

"Good idea."

"No one will miss it."

Over the next week they sent each other long emails detailing various ideas and plots to steal the stone.

Several were quite scary and a few involved violence.

Rock considered them all and chose the best.

{"You'll need to break in late over the weekend. Soon"}

"Perhaps after all it would be easiest to break in over the weekend," suggested Kamal.

{"Good, idea."}

"Good idea," said Barry. "Let's go ahead with that plan."
Rock sent further directions.

§

"We should break in on Sunday evening and smash it to pieces," said Barry. "She'll never know it was us. We'll take most of the pieces. The rest won't be any use to her broken and she'll throw them out. Then we can deconstruct it and work out how to build new components like it."

{"You got it! About time!"}

After some minor adjustments, it was organised for that Sunday.
Barry headed the planning. He pushed away any possibility of it being wrong.
"Stop worrying Kamal. It's just a question of obtaining research material. Lucia has no right to it. She probably appropriated it from somewhere illegal. I don't believe a word of her story about its origins. As for Terry claiming its millions of years old? Hah! We'll soon be able to disprove that!"

3.

Kamal (who headed a research group into search engines for internet servers) met Barry. The time was set for 8:00 pm, at the usual local.

He wasn't clear on the details. But Barry had bullied him into submission.

His research student, Ian, tagged along, bearing a climbing pick and rucksack. He was the patsy, in case the plan went wrong.

The pub was quiet, almost deserted.

Eric the Barman already knew them from their monthly meetings and tried to eavesdrop in on their mysterious whispers.

He nodded to Tom, the washer up.

"Those three are up to something,"

After downing several stiff drinks, the conspirators tiptoed across the road to the university.

"Look at them," said Eric.

He pulled back the heavy velvet curtains which obscured day light, and gave the bar its requisite dusk like atmosphere.

"Might as well be wearing striped shirts, berets and masks," said Tom, wiping his hands on his dirty jeans. "They're off to nick something, innit?"

They certainly looked suspicious, peering around surreptitiously, carrying an empty rucksack and what looked like a jemmy.

§

The weekend porter signed them in and handed over the master keys without comment.

"They look a bit peculiar," he thought mildly, "still; Sunday's a day when mostly freaks attend college."

He cast a glance over their outrageous hair.

"Yup. Freak-day all right," he said to himself. He was watching the rugby.

He turned back to his tiny screen and forgot about them.

Their guilty footsteps reverberated through the deserted halls of Learning, past empty lecture theatres, brim-full of slumbering equipment winking away, ready to re-initialise at the hint of movement.

They passed by silent rooms, still haunted by shades of Knowledge, and a handful of students rushing to finish courseworks due on Monday at

9.00am.

A few lecturers were in, even on Sunday evening - the college 'ghosts'.

Ian knocked over a bin outside someone's office and nearly gave Kamal a heart attack.

The crash reverberated through the empty corridors.

No one opened their doors. No one seemed to be around.

The conspirators reached the offices on the fourth floor and opened Lucia's office using the master key.

The keys jangled eerily in the hallway. Kamal was sweating profusely, and Ian had a sickly greenish pallor.

Providentially, there was no surveillance on office floors.

The door to the fourth floor opened with a creak. They closed it behind them.

Click.

It sounded loud in the empty, echoing building.

Ian jumped at the sound. Kamal looked very uneasy.

"Stop being so nervous! It's a fool-proof plan. Our presence here will be untraceable," Barry reassured his recalcitrant co-conspirators "we just open the filing cabinet, remove the rock and smash it to pieces."

Kamal whined. "But it's so beautiful."

"Stop being so sentimental. We'll leave a few bits on the floor. She'll assume that the rock spontaneously exploded and smashed the lock."

Ian, a gangly lanky haired nerd, giggled uncertainly. He'd never done anything like this before and was worried he would throw up.

Barry turned the key to Lucia's office. They got into the room without any difficulty.

It was dark.

They didn't dare turn the light on. Luckily it was dimly lit from the street.

A faint buzz emanated from the filing cabinet.

Ian stepped back, arms up, head circling like a meerkat suspecting a predator. The buzzing noise sounded aware - even prescient.

Barry looked at him condescendingly.

"Students," he murmured, "no backbone."

As high priest of the cult of science, he ignored the statically charged atmosphere and pushed Ian to the fore. *He* wasn't afraid. His deity, Science, could successfully explain any phenomenon – including the essence of life.

He stood behind Ian barking orders.

"Move on there! It's nothing."

Ian stood there paralysed with fear.

Barry hissed angrily and snatched the ice-pick from him. He forced open the filing cabinet with a jarring clatter.

Ian jerked forward and pulled out the Rock. He received a static shocked and dropped it on the floor.

He stood there, trembling uselessly. He'd heard weird rumours about the rock.

"It's alive!"

The globe before them glowed and clicked. It sparked with blue lights and minute jolts of electricity snaked across it surface.

Rock braced itself for the next phase. It created fault lines and initialised various new components, sending them data and instructions.

On the floor below, a fellow lecturer was at work. The windows were open. They could hear him sputtering to himself in the sudden stillness.

"That's Dave," said Kamal. "Do you think he can hear us?"

"Of course not," said Barry.

Dave was *always* in. He was playing a multiplayer game, shouting something into his headphones about Russians. (As he later told the investigators, "I heard nothing.")

Kamal and Ian clung as close to the door as possible.

The hum from the rock was growing very audible indeed.

Lucia's computer turned itself on. A new translation typed itself on screen and the printer began to spew out paper.

Barry turned the screen off.

There was a pause.

Neither Ian nor Kamal moved.

Barry tutted disdainfully and grabbed the rock from the floor. Another pause as Ian shuffled forward, driven by Kamal's elbow in the small of his back. Barry handed him the ice pick.

Ian struck at the stone limply, hoping to miss.

The last thing anyone remembered was a flash of blue as it fell neatly into curiously geometric segments.

§

No one except Lucia had seen it adapt before. It turned and twisted like a multi-hedronal Rubik's cube. It had no pathetic 128-bit registers but was a rotating cube with multiple axes. A mass of interconnected and co-operating parts adjusted. Each component could conjoin with others if need be, depending on the type of problem.

There was a subsonic screech as multiple sub-systems adjusted to the situation. It sparkled and glowed, shimmering with energy.

If only it were possible for the engineers to see it!

Tiny systems scurried across the room and under doors to access the server nodes and travel along cables, while others combined to form curious geometric shapes and lumbered off slowly.

§

On the floor below, Dave's on-line computer game went pixelated and slowed to a grinding halt. He thumped the computer and yelled in frustration.

It came back instantly.

He smiled to himself in satisfaction,

"Sometimes, shouting at the system works."

§

The hum in Lucia's office was deafening for a while. Then it subsided. The engineers lay there, as their spinal cortex was infested, and their neural operating systems were modified.

The rock whined with glee. It had never been able to perform such radical changes to the human brain before. It couldn't wait to take control.

§

Dave played DotA until 3.00am, when his US co-players went off line and headed for school.

He walked home to the halls of residence where he looked after first years (who had never seen him). He slept till midday on Monday, flung on his clothes, which had started to smell a bit rank, and returned to work.

As a result, he missed all the fun.

Continued
in
Book Two of the Terraform Trilogy:

Defenders

About Tereska Karran
Ba Hons, PGCE, MA, PgDip, PgDip, MSc, PhD

Tereska is an author and artist.
She has two websites
https://ArtbyTereskaKarran.com
https://StreetPublishing.co.uk.
She has written several books:

Science Fiction:

The Terraform Trilogy (which consists of four books)
Analysis of a Natural Terraform (A.N.T.)
Defenders
Origins
Redemption

Chronicles of the Dark Ages
The Toltechs
Shaders

Historical Fiction:

The Spoils of War
Shadow of the Zenana

Academic Non-Fiction:

An Architecture for Artificial Intelligence
Monetary Value in Virtual Transactions

Art and Poetry:

The Book of Hours

Facebook
Art by Tereska Karran
Writing by Tereska Karran

Twitter:
@ArtbyTereskaKarran
@WritingbyTereskaKarran

www.ingramcontent.com/pod-product-compliance
Lightning Source LLC
Chambersburg PA
CBHW060129130626
46556CB00006B/2287